THE TWIN DILEMMA

NANCY DREW MYSTERY STORIES®

THE TWIN DILEMMA

by
Carolyn Keene

Illustrated by
Paul Frame

WANDERER BOOKS
Published by Simon & Schuster, New York

Published by WANDERER BOOKS
A Simon & Schuster Division of
Gulf & Western Corporation
Simon & Schuster Building
1230 Avenue of the Americas
New York, New York 10020

Manufactured in the United States of America
10 9 8 7 6 5 4 3 2 1

NANCY DREW and NANCY DREW MYSTERY STORIES
are trademarks of Stratemeyer Syndicate,
registered in the United States Patent
and Trademark Office

WANDERER and colophon are trademarks of Simon & Schuster

Library of Congress Cataloging in Publication Data

Keene, Carolyn
The twin dilemma

(Nancy Drew mystery stories; 63)
Summary: When a model disappears, Nancy takes
her place in a benefit fashion show and helps to track down a dress thief.
[1. Mystery and detective stories. 2. Fashion—
Fiction] I. Frame, Paul, 1913- ill. II. Title.
III. Series: Keene, Carolyn. Nancy Drew mystery
stories; 63.
PZ7.K23   Nan no. 63   [Fic]   81-11560
ISBN 0-671-42358-4   AACR2
ISBN 0-671-42359-2 (pbk.)

Contents

1

The Missing Model

"Nancy!" Eloise Drew exclaimed happily as she opened the door of her apartment. "Am I glad you're here!"

"That makes two of us, Aunt Eloise," the eighteen-year-old said. "I mean, four of us!"

The young detective gestured toward her friends, Bess Marvin and George Fayne, who were dragging large suitcases down the carpeted hallway.

"You didn't know we planned to stay in New York forever," Nancy said teasingly as the girls set the luggage down in the apartment.

Aunt Eloise laughed. "I hope you're as well prepared for the assignment I have for you as you seem to be with all that luggage you brought along. It's a model mystery."

There was a glint of mischief in her doe-brown eyes as she noticed her niece's bewilderment. Nancy was the daughter of Carson Drew, Aunt Eloise's brother, a well-known attorney in River Heights. Nancy had frequently assisted him on cases and had gained a substantial reputation for herself as an amateur detective.

Bess and George looked surprised as well. "I thought we were here to see a benefit fashion show and have a fun vacation," Bess said, poking a strand of blond hair behind her ear.

"Is that where the model mystery is?" George asked. Unlike her plump cousin, Bess, she was tall and slim with dark hair cropped fairly short.

"Yes and no," Aunt Eloise replied. "Remember, I told you I'm involved in running a benefit fashion show? Well, one of our models has disappeared. She wasn't at the rehearsal today, and she isn't at home. Nobody seems to know where she went. Jacqueline Henri is her name. Perhaps you've heard of her."

"Oh, she's gorgeous," Bess swooned. "Bony thin with fabulous black hair and violet eyes. She's been on the covers of lots of magazines. I'd love to meet her!"

"I was planning to introduce you tonight—"

"What if we can't find her before the show starts?" Nancy said, assuming that the search was the assignment her aunt had mentioned.

"You'll be stuck without a model," George said to Nancy's aunt.

"No, I won't," Eloise Drew said. "If you promise not to disappear on me, too, Nancy, I'd like you to stand in for Jacqueline."

"Me? Oh, I couldn't!" the girl protested.

"Sure you could," Bess spoke up. "You've done modeling before."

"But only at the Woman's Club," Nancy said. "Besides, how could I possibly wear clothes meant for Jacqueline Henri? She must be thinner than I am, and we don't have the same coloring."

"Not much thinner," Aunt Eloise said, stepping back to look at the girl. "And your coloring is fine, too. You'll see."

"But what about Jacqueline?" Nancy asked.

Her aunt pursed her lips. "I don't know what to think. Marjorie Tyson, my co-chairman, has been trying to track her down ever since this morning."

"Maybe something happened to her," Bess commented.

"Or maybe she's just unreliable," her cousin added.

"Well, I don't want you girls to trouble yourselves about her until after the show," Aunt Eloise said. "We expect to have more than five hundred people in the audience and we can't disappoint them."

Although the program was still several hours away, the visitors quickly freshened up and changed. Aunt Eloise made a number of telephone calls, and when she finally laid down the receiver, she sighed happily.

"It's all arranged. We have to get over to the hotel as soon as possible," the woman said, ducking her head into the girls' room. "Mr. Reese—"

"Richard Reese, the famous designer?" Bess interrupted.

Aunt Eloise nodded. "He needs to see you for a fitting, Nancy."

"I'm almost ready," the young detective said, fumbling nervously with the zipper of a long, emerald-green taffeta skirt.

"Very pretty, dear," her aunt replied, "but why not carry it with you? You can change for the party after the show."

"Oh, you're right," Nancy said while Bess and George helped each other fasten tiny hooks on their gowns.

"Come on, slowpoke," George teased Nancy

as she slipped out of the skirt into another and kicked off her satin shoes in favor of leather heels.

She put everything into a garment bag with pockets for accessories, then joined the others in the living room. Bess giggled while George stepped toward Nancy, her eyes clearly fixed on the girl's titian head.

"What's so funny?" Nancy asked.

George removed a hairclip that had pinned back an unruly curl.

"The stylist will fix your hair," Aunt Eloise assured her niece as they left.

The girls didn't discuss the model again until their cab cut across Fifth Avenue toward Rockefeller Center. It came to a halt for a few moments while two limousines merged into the line of traffic, giving Nancy and the others a chance to study the crowd who watched the skaters in the rink below. They were gliding in tempo to a familiar melody.

As the cab started to move again, Nancy and Bess, who was nearest the window, noticed an attractive young woman among the pedestrians on Fifth Avenue. She wore a dappled fur coat and a hat to match that barely covered a thick mane of ebony hair.

"It's Jacqueline Henri!" Bess cried, as the

model darted to the corner of the block behind them.

"Are you sure?" Nancy asked.

"Positive."

Instantly, Aunt Eloise, who was squeezed tightly between the girls, reached for the cab door.

"Please stop," she told the driver, but retracted the request when she observed Jacqueline stepping into a cab that was evidently headed downtown, away from their destination.

"We couldn't catch her if we tried," she concluded.

"Does Jacqueline live around here?" Nancy inquired.

"On the other side of Rockefeller Center, near Broadway, I think," Aunt Eloise answered. "Perhaps she had trouble getting a taxi up there and decided to walk until she found one."

"At least we know she's all right," Bess said.

"Aunt Eloise, you said people were trying to track her down all day," Nancy commented. "Did anyone actually go to her apartment?"

"Probably not. Everybody's been terribly busy at the hotel ballroom."

"Does Miss Henri have an answering service?" Nancy went on.

"Oh, yes. I'd venture to say every working model does."

"But she didn't leave a message?" George put in.

"No. There was no explanation for her absence whatsoever."

"That's strange," Nancy said. "Seems to me that she didn't become a top model by being irresponsible. And yet, she's obviously in town. She could have called."

They rode in silence until they reached the hotel. By now the last glimmer of sun had faded between the tall buildings, and there was only a residue of dusky glow when the girls got out of the cab and smiled at the doorman under the gold canopy.

Nancy took a deep breath as he opened the door, admitting the visitors to an elegant, wood-paneled lobby. Aunt Eloise led the way past velvet ottomans to a room adjacent to the dining area. It was filled with clothing racks.

"I can't wait to see everything," Bess sighed, watching a girl pull a soft coral-colored pants suit off one of the racks. "Which outfits will Nancy be wearing?"

George noticed a sheer turquoise dress on the same rack marked REESE. "That one, maybe?" she said.

"No," Aunt Eloise replied. "Because of the switch in models, Mr. Reese has made a few changes in his selection. Follow me, everybody."

"Suppose Jacqueline shows up in time?" Nancy asked.

"She'll be out of luck," Aunt Eloise said firmly. "We won't rearrange everything again at the last minute."

She stepped across the room and introduced the girls to Marjorie Tyson, a petite woman with short, gray hair that framed her thin, lively face.

"Am I glad you're here!" she greeted Nancy, causing the girls to laugh.

"That's what Aunt Eloise said, Miss Tyson," Nancy explained. Then she told the woman about the model they had spotted at Rockefeller Center.

"Well, if she comes now, she'll be too late," Miss Tyson said, agreeing with Aunt Eloise's decision. "And please call me Marjorie. Nancy, the dresses you'll be modeling are over there. Bess and George, do you mind waiting while I take Nancy to a dressing alcove? There's a bench for you in the corner."

"Of course not," Bess replied and Marjorie

strode toward the rack of clothes. Then she gaped in shock.

"There are only a few outfits left! I wonder what happened to the rest."

Suddenly, a man in a turtleneck sweater and jeans appeared from behind a screen carrying an empty box. He dumped it on the floor, his face a contortion of rage.

"They're gone! Every last one gone!" he shouted angrily.

"But what about these?" Marjorie said, touching one of the pastel gowns on the rack.

"Never mind these," he roared. "They're the ones the thief left!" With that, he snapped them off the metal hanger and stormed past the two women.

"Mr. Reese!" Majorie pleaded. "Please tell us what's going to happen. This is Nancy Drew, Jackie's replacement. She's all ready to—"

"Forget it!" the designer snapped. "I don't care who she is. All I know is that my clothes are gone!

2

Design Scoop!

The force of his words made Nancy flinch. She knew it was futile to try to stop the man. He had already ignored Marjorie Tyson and was marching forward, blinded by the puffed sleeves of an organza dress he was clutching tightly.

"Out of my way!" he bellowed at no one in particular.

But it was too late! Bess and George, who had left their seats to talk with Aunt Eloise, were just crossing the room in front of him. He crashed into them, causing them to stumble in different directions. Mr. Reese himself tripped over the metal foot of the rack, and fell headlong into the clothes that hung on it, ripping them off hangers.

"Oh, Mr. Reese!" Marjorie squealed, running to help the man up.

Aunt Eloise and the girls joined her, but he refused their assistance. He sputtered as he tried to get to his feet, then slipped on the hem of a satin skirt and wound up on the floor again.

The young detectives tried to keep from laughing, but the designer heard Bess's giggle and gritted his teeth. He flung the satin skirt aside, clearing his path at last. When he stood up to face Miss Tyson and Aunt Eloise, he glared at them.

"I should never have listened to Sheila," he complained.

"Who's Sheila?" George whispered.

"Maybe his wife?" Bess guessed, as the girls picked up the fallen clothes and hung them on the rack.

"Those don't belong there," Mr. Reese snarled, pointing to the four outfits he had held in his arms before he fell. "Can't you read?"

The sign on the rack said STEINER, referring to another designer in the fashion show.

"Did you want to leave your things on the floor?" a voice from behind them asked.

It belonged to a woman who wore a smock and a pincushion on her wrist that contained plenty of needles.

"And you're fired, Rosalind!" he growled back, sending the woman into a flood of tears.

"You can't walk out on us now," Aunt Eloise begged him.

"What do you mean I can't? I can and I am."

"Mr. Reese," Nancy interrupted in the sweetest tone she could muster, "perhaps I can be of help. I'm a detective."

He looked at the girl, his expression changing dramatically. He gave a war whoop and laughed loudly.

"Sure. And I'm the Emperor of China!"

Bess and George bit their lips to keep from saying something they might regret later.

"Nancy *is* a detective." Aunt Eloise defended her niece.

"Of course, maybe Mr. Reese doesn't need a detective," Nancy challenged. "He hasn't told us yet what his problem is!"

"I'll tell you what I need—a bodyguard for my clothes!" he stated flatly. "The ones I selected for you, Miss Drew, were taken."

"Stolen?" George asked.

"Exactly."

"What makes you so positive they were stolen?" Nancy inquired. Then, seeing the irritation grow in his face, she quickly changed the question. "Might they have been misplaced?"

19

"No. I personally rode over here with everything, and up until an hour ago when I had to make a phone call, I did not leave this room."

As he talked, Nancy walked toward two chairs, leaving her friends to discuss the situation among themselves. By now, the man's temper had subsided and he followed her, anxious to know her thoughts on the situation.

"It was all Sheila's idea—my wife's," he said. "She's involved in practically every charity in New York, including this one. She asked me if I'd mind showing a few of the new spring designs before their official debut. Well, I said I would look over the lot and pull what I could for this show."

"How many outfits in all?" Nancy questioned.

"In the spring collection or for this show only?"

"For this show."

"Seven."

"There were four in the alcove," Nancy muttered, "so three are missing."

"That's right."

"I still don't understand, though, how they could've disappeared without someone seeing the thief."

"I can't figure it out, either." The designer

20

moaned. "I'll have to leave that mystery up to you."

The girl detective had only been in New York a short time and already she had encountered two mysteries—Jacqueline Henri's strange behavior and the theft of the Reese creations.

Out of the corner of her eye she noticed Aunt Eloise checking her watch. The fashion show was scheduled to begin in fewer than forty-five minutes, and Nancy wondered how they would compensate for the missing portion of the program.

Richard Reese saw the anxiety in her eyes, cleared his throat several times, and finally spoke. "You're not Jacqueline, but you'll do."

"You mean it?" Nancy gasped in excitement. "You'll let me model your clothes?"

He nodded, somewhat embarrassed, then regained his composure and ordered her into the dressing alcove.

"Rosalind?" he called out, but there was no response. "Where is she?" he asked Marjorie Tyson.

"You fired her, remember?"

"Oh, that's ridiculous," Mr. Reese said. "She knows I have a bad temper."

Even so, his assistant did not return and another young woman was asked to help out.

"This is Yolanda. She's one of our stylists and she will help you dress," the designer announced. "We don't have much time left and I must fit you before you go onstage."

It was decided that instead of introducing the program, Nancy would be third.

"Good luck—I mean, break a leg," George told her friend as she and Bess excused themselves to find their table in the ballroom.

Nancy, however, was busy listening to instructions from the designer and did not hear the girls say good-bye. She was quickly hurried behind the screen in the dressing room and handed a softly ruffled, blue silk blouse and a matching skirt with a short linen jacket.

I hope it fits, she murmured to herself, fastening the skirt waist. It was snug, but not uncomfortable. Then came the jacket over the blouse. The sleeves slid over her arms easily and, to her relief, the cuff length was perfect. She stepped out in front of the mirror, letting Yolanda tug and smooth the clothes until they hung neatly.

"Now the hair," the stylist said. She pulled a brush out of a pocket and swept it through Nancy's titian waves. "We want a natural look," she said as she finished, and then led her to Mr. Reese.

"Wonderful!" he exclaimed, then asked Nancy to walk the length of the room. "Just relax," he told her. "Now turn and come back."

The grin on his face proved that he was pleased with her performance. A few moments later, he escorted her to the stage, leaving her to wait for her cue.

"The spring season would not be complete . . ." Nancy heard the hostess say into the microphone, and she felt someone nudge her onto the runway.

Lights flashed around the ballroom as the girl detective posed in front of the curtain for a few seconds. The hostess, a striking woman in a glittering sequined gown, smiled at Nancy, motioning her to move forward.

"The jacket is reversible," she told the audience, something Nancy had not even noticed. The girl opened the jacket to reveal the lining and was about to remove it when Mr. Reese suddenly bolted toward the microphone.

"Leave, Miss Drew!" he shouted. "Get off the stage—now!"

Nancy blinked her eyes, momentarily stunned. Surely he wasn't serious, she thought, and remaining poised, she turned on her heels and walked back to the curtain.

"I am very sorry about this, ladies and gentlemen," he said, "but I must remove my designs from this program! I have been robbed!"

The hostess quickly cupped her hand over the microphone, begging him to say no more. He shrugged, then grabbed Nancy's arm and pulled her offstage. "I should never have listened to you," he snapped.

Nancy stared at him, openmouthed. "What happened?"

Mr. Reese hurried her back to the dressing room and pointed to a large catalog that bore the name Millington.

"Look at it," he told the girl.

Nancy leafed through the book, unsure of what she was supposed to find. It contained a variety of items, mostly clothing.

"Stop there," Mr. Reese said as she turned to a page near the end.

By now Bess and George had made their way into the dressing room, wondering anxiously what had caused the latest disruption. Aunt Eloise and Marjorie Tyson, on the other hand, had darted behind the stage to soothe the nerves of the next model.

"I think Reese is a bit daffy," Marjorie confided to Aunt Eloise. "The way he blows hot and cold, why, it's enough to drive anyone crazy!"

The designer, however, had not acted on an emotional whim when he took Nancy out of the fashion show. He had a very good reason, which he now explained to her.

"These dresses," he said, indicating pictures in the Millington catalog, "are copies of gowns I designed for this year's spring collection. They haven't even been shown in public yet!"

"It's not unusual, though, to see copies of originals, is it?" Bess asked.

"No, it isn't," the man replied with a steely glance at the girl. "But usually, and I stress the word usually, copies, or knock-offs, as we say in the industry, appear *after* the originals are shown, not before!"

Nancy raised her eyebrows. "You mean, someone actually scooped your designs?"

"That's right! Now none of my clients will buy my spring collection when they see copies of original dresses on every woman in the country!"

Reese clothing was very expensive, the girls knew, so the designer would probably lose a lot of income as a result.

"Is Millington a retail operation or a manufacturer of clothes?" Nancy asked.

"They're a manufacturer selling to big retailers all over the United States!" the designer explained. "Now do you see how serious this is?"

"Could you rustle up some new designs to replace the ones that were stolen?" Bess inquired timidly.

"Hardly. They take weeks, months, to create and execute!" Mr. Reese insisted. "No, I'm absolutely ruined!"

3

Stranger's Story

"But how could anyone get hold of your designs?" George asked Mr. Reese.

He had collapsed into a chair and buried his face in his hands. "I don't know, I don't know," he kept repeating. "We have very tight security in the office."

"Maybe that's part of the answer," Nancy said.

She was about to inquire into his staff but realized she ought to wait until after the fashion show. The sponsors had lost a precious contribution when the designer pulled out so abruptly, and she was determined to do all she could to reverse the effect.

"Please let me go on," Nancy begged the man.

"And have these clothes photographed for the Millington catalog, too? Never!"

"But the damage has already been done," Nancy said. She thrust the catalog under the man's nose and pointed to a picture of a skirt and jacket that closely resembled the one she wore.

"That's right," Aunt Eloise, who was standing in the doorway, chimed in. "Our patrons have paid a lot of money for their tickets, Mr. Reese, and to disrupt every—"

Her voice broke off as tears welled up in her eyes. She started to walk away when Marjorie Tyson strode past her, carrying a message.

"Maybe this will change your mind," she said confidently.

Mr. Reese glanced at the folded paper with disinterest.

"Please—read this," the woman persisted.

As he opened it, Nancy could not help seeing that it was a request to buy the same outfit she had modeled only a short while ago.

"Zoe Babbitt is an old customer of mine," the man mumbled, referring to the signature on the note.

"Then—" Nancy said hopefully.

"Yolanda, get the organza!" Mr. Reese demanded, and the stylist hurried off.

Instantly, Aunt Eloise threw her arms around his shoulders and planted a kiss on his cheek. "You're wonderful," she said gaily.

"Oh, stop it," he replied in embarrassment. "And hurry up!"

"Thank you," Aunt Eloise said quietly. She and Marjorie followed Bess and George back to the ballroom, leaving Nancy to attend to the next change of clothing.

As before, the second outfit fit almost perfectly. This time, however, Nancy winced as Yolanda drew the long zipper over her waist and up the back.

"Can you breathe?" Yolanda teased, noting the pinch in the midriff.

"Barely," Nancy replied hoarsely. She didn't dare relax for fear she would split a seam!

"What do you think, Mr. Reese?" Yolanda asked when the girl stood before him at last.

Instantly, he noticed the thin crease in the waistline, but a glance at his watch made him admit, "I'm afraid we haven't time to fix it." Then, as if a bolt of lightning had struck, he snapped his fingers. "Wait a minute," he said, and dived into a nearby box filled with assorted buttons and ribbons. He pulled out a long, wide band of grosgrain that was the same shade of lilac as the gown.

"Perfect," Yolanda said. She tied it into a pretty bow around the girl's waist, then quickly pinned Nancy's hair back, letting only a few wisps play against her cheekbones.

It was no surprise to either Mr. Reese or his assistant that the young model was greeted with loud applause. Nancy was stunning and sailed down the runway as if she had done it many times. The remaining two outfits, a tailored white suit and a silk hostess gown, were equally popular.

When Nancy stood at the end of the platform for the last time, a camera flashed in the back of the room, drawing her attention there. Not far from where the flash had come stood a woman in a dappled fur coat thrown casually over her shoulders.

That looks like Jacqueline Henri, Nancy thought. She was tempted to stare, but forced herself to turn instead and walk slowly toward the curtain where she posed once more before exiting.

"Wasn't she marvelous?" the hostess said to the audience over the microphone, bringing another round of applause for Nancy.

But the girl detective heard only an echo of it as she rushed back to the dressing room to change into her own skirt and blouse. She wondered if Bess and George had spotted the model, too. However, before she could consider the possibility further, she found herself surrounded by Mr. Reese and several young women. All of them complimented her profusely.

"Miss Drew," Mr. Reese said with an air of formality, "will you help me find the thieves?"

"I was just about to ask you for your business card," Nancy replied, smiling.

She pulled away long enough to slip into the clothes she had brought from Aunt Eloise's, then emerged to face Mr. Reese once again.

"Where are you running to, Nancy?" he asked inquisitively, adding, "I'd like to talk with you if you can spare a minute."

Nancy glanced past the man in preoccupation. She was eager to find Jacqueline Henri but decided not to mention anything to Mr. Reese.

"Perhaps we could discuss the theft tomorrow," she suggested, smiling politely.

"I may have to leave on business," was the reply. "Can't we—"

The girl detective broke in gently. "On second thought," she said, "I wonder if you would draw me some rough sketches of the dresses that were stolen tonight."

"Of course, I'd be glad to, but—"

"And jot down the type of material you used for each one," Nancy concluded. "Now, I really must get back to the ballroom."

As she hurried toward the corridor, Mr. Reese told her he would have the sketches ready by morning.

"Great," Nancy called back. Her feet picked up speed as the sound of music drifted into the lobby, but when she stepped into the ballroom, she halted immediately.

What if Jacqueline had left? She trained her vision on the couples who were dancing, then shifted it to the tables. Bess and George waved to her, but Nancy did not see them. Instead, she was struck by the sight of a dappled fur coat on a nearby chair.

That's Jacquel—Nancy gasped to herself when the young woman seemed to appear from nowhere.

"Miss Henri!" Nancy exclaimed, running to her. "We've been worried sick about you."

The puzzled expression that greeted her prompted Nancy to explain the comment. She introduced herself as Eloise Drew's niece.

"I tried to be here on time for the show," Jacqueline said, "but couldn't make it. I phoned your aunt, but she had already left."

"I'm sure she'd like to talk to you now," Nancy said. "She—" Her sentence was interrupted by an announcement over the loudspeaker.

"Will Jacqueline Henri please come to the desk."

The young woman looked worried and tense. "That's for me," she said. "I'll have to go now."

"Is something the matter?" Nancy asked, sensing that there was.

"No—I'll call your aunt tomorrow." But before the model was able to excuse herself, Bess and George had joined the two.

"Oh, Miss Henri! It's a pleasure to meet you!" Bess called out, extending her hand at the same time. Jacqueline's was cold and clammy. "Wasn't Nancy wonderful?" Bess rambled on until her cousin spoke.

"We wondered what had happened to you," George said. "Why didn't you come to work?"

"I—I couldn't," Jacqueline said. "Something terrible happened and—" She broke off and started to turn away from the trio.

Nancy gently put her hand on the model's arm. "Maybe we can help?"

Jackie shook her head. "No, you can't," she answered. "It's about my brother. He may have been kidnapped!"

4

Studio Clue

"Kidnapped! Are you sure?" Nancy asked.

Again the call came over the loudspeaker, interrupting the model before she could reply.

"Miss Jacqueline Henri, will Miss Jacqueline Henri please come to the desk," the voice repeated.

"I'll be back," she told the girls abruptly and walked away.

"If she believes her brother was kidnapped," George said, "what's she doing here?"

"Maybe *he* was supposed to be here," Nancy suggested, glancing in the direction of the lobby.

The hotel desk was not visible from where the girls stood and Nancy wondered how much longer it would be before the young woman returned.

"Maybe she said that only to keep us from following her," George remarked after several minutes.

"Come on," Nancy said, leading the two cousins across the corridor. "Let's see if we can find her."

As they stepped into the main lobby, they were astonished by the number of people with suitcases crowding the registration area.

"They must've come in on a late plane," Nancy observed.

"Or a bus," George said, directing everyone's attention to a man in a driver's uniform.

He pushed his way through the crowd, waving his hands and talking at the same time. The hubbub dissipated as the group huddled around him.

"I don't see Jacqueline anywhere," Bess commented.

"She could've met someone and left," Nancy said, and hurried toward one of the desk clerks, asking if he knew where the stunning, black-haired woman had gone.

"I haven't seen her at all," the young man replied, "and from your description, I'm sure I'd remember her."

Then, on a sudden thought, she approached the bus driver. He had been outside the hotel when Jacqueline left, if, in fact, she had. But to Nancy's chagrin, the man said he had not seen her, either.

"Let's go back to the ballroom," Nancy said. "I'm sure Aunt Eloise is wondering what has happened to us."

As the trio weaved between tables, several patrons stopped Nancy, complimenting her performance and the gowns she had worn.

"Absolutely exquisite," someone said from behind, causing Nancy to turn toward the dance floor. "Miss Drew?" The young man who spoke stepped closer, aligning himself under the soft light of a chandelier.

Nancy judged him to be in his thirties, despite the deep lines under his gray eyes. "Did you say something?" Nancy asked.

"I was just about to invite you to dance," came the unexpected reply.

The orchestra was switching tempos and Nancy nodded. She followed the stranger to the center of the floor where several other couples were trying unsuccessfully to keep from bumping into each other.

"I don't know your name," the young detective said as the two began to dance.

"It's Chris," he said. "Chris Chavez. You took

Jacqueline Henri's place on the program, didn't you?"

"Mm-hmm," Nancy replied casually. "Do you know her?"

"Doesn't everyone?"

"I guess so."

Chris swirled her away from him, but held her hand firmly, drawing her back.

"Do you do a lot of modeling?" he inquired.

"As a matter of fact," Nancy said, "this is the first time I've done anything like this. I've modeled before, but not on this scale."

"That's really hard to believe. You looked so professional up on that runway," Chris went on. Despite the dim light, he could see the blush in Nancy's cheeks. "I hope I'm not embarrassing you," he said.

"Oh, no," the girl said, starting to giggle. "I was just thinking how happy it would make our housekeeper if I changed careers."

Her dance partner appeared bewildered. "What's your current occupation?" he asked as the music finished at last.

"I'm a detective," Nancy said. Now it was her turn to watch for a change of expression, but to her surprise, there was none. Chris made no comment. Instead, he trailed her to the table where Bess and George sat with Aunt Eloise and Marjorie Tyson, and Nancy introduced him to her friends.

"Not *the* Chris Chavez." Marjorie grinned. "The photographer?"

Chris nodded. "And I'd like to take a picture of Nancy in that gorgeous gown she wore earlier."

"Well, I'm sure that can be arranged," Aunt Eloise said enthusiastically.

Bess, meanwhile, tugged on Nancy's arm. "George and I were wondering where you went," she whispered. "We didn't realize you had met such a handsome man. Does he have a couple of friends?"

"I don't know. Shall I ask?" Nancy replied.

The blond girl giggled while the young photographer jotted down his phone number and handed it to Nancy. "I'll be at the studio tomorrow, so let me know if you can come by," he said, then walked off quickly.

"What will Ned think when he sees you on the cover of some famous magazine—and photographed by the world-famous Chris Chavez?" George teased Nancy.

"Ned Nickerson," Nancy replied, referring to her boyfriend from Emerson College, "won't think anything because he won't see any such thing."

"Want to bet?" Bess winked.

"It's not so farfetched, Nancy," her aunt said instantly. "You could become a top model like Jacqueline."

"But I don't want to be," Nancy declared. "I'm very happy doing what I do. Which reminds me—what do you know about Jacqueline Henri? I assume Bess and George told you about our encounter with her."

"Yes, they did," Marjorie said. "I really don't know very much about her. You should have asked Chris."

Chris! Nancy thought, irritated that she had literally let him slip through her fingers.

"I'm going to call him in a little while," she declared.

"You are?" Bess repeated. "But it's after midnight."

"He only left a few minutes ago, so I'll try his house in half an hour," Nancy decided.

The ballroom had begun to empty as Nancy made her way down the quiet hallway to a phone booth not far from the dressing room. The overhead lights had been turned off, but the sconces on the wall were still lit.

Nancy gasped as the silhouette of a man played across a distant, smoke-colored mirror. She ducked into the booth, waiting for the stranger to show himself.

Where's the security guard? Nancy wondered, suddenly aware that the precious designer clothes had been left unprotected. Although chains had been strung through the garments and locked, the girl detective knew that a professional thief wouldn't be easily discouraged.

Now the mysterious figure hurried across the room to the door, as if he suddenly realized he had left it open by accident. Nancy stuck her head out at the same moment, linking eyes with him!

He had small, even features, and despite the streak of gray in his hair, he looked fairly young. He also wore a tuxedo, causing Nancy to assume that he had attended the fashion show.

"Who are you and what are you doing in here?" she asked boldly.

The intruder responded with a cold, angry stare. He strode past the girl, not saying a word. She decided to postpone her phone call to Chris, and dashed quickly into the dressing room. So far as she could tell, nothing had been disturbed, but before she returned to her table, she reported the incident to the hotel desk.

"Perhaps the man was just an interested admirer," Aunt Eloise told Nancy when she related the story. "It doesn't pay to be too suspicious, dear."

The young detective would have been the first to agree under other circumstances, but she did not argue the point. As it was, she barely could keep her eyes open on the way back to the apartment.

In spite of her exhaustion, however, Nancy tossed restlessly. Who was Jacqueline's brother and why did the young model imagine he had been kidnapped? The same questions rose in her mind as she awoke the next morning.

Before I do anything, though, I'm going to call Dad, Nancy decided.

She dressed quickly and joined her aunt and the other girls at the breakfast table, where they planned the itinerary for the day, beginning with phone calls home and one to Chris Chavez, who invited them to come to his studio later that morning.

Then, leaving Aunt Eloise, who was to meet Marjorie Tyson at the hotel office, the young detectives headed for Mr. Reese's. Nancy was not entirely surprised to learn that he wasn't there.

"He is flying to Palm Beach today," the receptionist said, "but he left this envelope for you, Miss Drew."

Nancy opened it immediately, discovering several sketches of the missing gowns, along with other pertinent information.

"When will he be back?" Nancy inquired.

"Tomorrow, perhaps."

"There are too many disappearing acts around here to suit me," Bess whispered to George.

"You can say that again," her cousin replied. "I think—"

"Let's go," Nancy interrupted, and turned to leave. "Our next stop is the studio of Chris Chavez!"

On the way, she studied Mr. Reese's sketches, almost memorizing them, and advised Bess and George to do the same.

"If only one of these gowns turned up in my closet, I'd be thrilled!" Bess said, as their taxi halted in front of a seemingly deserted store. "Is this the studio?"

"Guess so," Nancy said as they stepped out.

The chill in the air had left a thin layer of frost

on the window, so the visitors could not see inside. The door was open, though, and they entered.

"Anybody home?" Nancy called out across the empty foyer.

No one answered.

At the end of the hall was another door and an unshaded lamp shone brightly.

"Somebody must be here," Bess commented, walking forward. Nancy and George followed.

Suddenly, two voices rose in argument and the hall door slammed shut!

5

The Lion's Message

Nancy and the cousins listened to the angry voices behind the closed door.

"Ted Henri can take care of himself," the man, apparently Chris, was saying to someone.

He must be talking about Jacqueline's brother! Nancy thought, and knocked on the door.

Bess was apprehensive. "Shall we wait for you outside?" she whispered to her friend, not wishing to get caught in the middle of the strangers' argument.

To her chagrin, however, Nancy shook her head. "I might need your help."

"But—" Bess mumbled as the voices subsided and the door opened, revealing an unexpected surprise. A young woman stood before them with Chris Chavez, who was looking over her shoulder.

"Jacqueline!" Nancy exclaimed.

"Oh, so you know each other," Chris interposed.

"We met last evening," Nancy said, adding pointedly, "When you didn't come back, Jackie, we were worried."

"I'm terribly sorry," the model apologized. "I was so tired that I left the hotel after I took my message." She paused, turning to Chris. "Nancy is a detective, you know."

"Yes, I do," the photographer said. He kept his eyes evenly fixed on Nancy. "I imagine Jackie has told you about her brother."

"Not really," Nancy said. "Who *is* your brother?" the girl detective went on.

"Ted's a journalist—an investigative reporter," Jacqueline said, then stopped as if wondering how much to reveal.

"Go ahead," Chris urged her. "Tell Nancy everything. She may be able to help you."

The young woman's cheeks flushed. "I don't really know where to begin," she said. "As I told you last night, I believe my brother may have been kidnapped."

"But you're not sure," Nancy said.

"I'm almost sure. It's not the first time he's

been threatened. In the course of his job, he has exposed numerous undercover schemes and stepped on lots of toes."

"But what makes you think he was kidnapped?" Nancy questioned.

"For one thing, he was supposed to arrive on a charter flight from Singapore yesterday evening. I got a cable to meet him at Kennedy Airport. That's why I couldn't be in the fashion show. Anyway, when I reached the airport, I couldn't find him."

"Was he on the passenger list?" Nancy asked.

"As far as I know."

"Then, are you suggesting he may have been abducted from the airport?"

Jacqueline shook her head. "I don't know what to think," she said. "When I went home, I found this in my mailbox." She dug into her purse and produced a piece of paper.

On it was written a message with some scribbling at the bottom that resembled a lion's crest. Nancy read the message aloud:

IF YOU DON'T HEAR FROM ME IN A FEW DAYS, CALL THE POLICE. DON'T TRY TO CONTACT ME BEFORE THEN.   T.

The girl glanced at Jacqueline. "Is this your brother's handwriting?"

"I'm not sure. It may be a good imitation. That's why I'm so afraid he might have been kidnapped."

"Suppose he did write the note," Nancy said. "I assume the 'T' stands for Ted. But what's this funny symbol next to it? It looks like the head of a lion."

"I don't know," Jackie said.

"You see," Chris spoke up, "Ted's been working on an important exposé about a fake operation at an auction house."

"I don't think we should talk about that," Jacqueline interrupted. "I'm sure Ted wouldn't appreciate it."

"Why not? If Nancy is to help you, she has to know what's going on." The young man paused a moment, then continued. "It seems that some auction house here in Manhattan has sold spurious reproductions of antique jewelry to a number of people, including dealers."

"But surely they would know the real stuff from the fake," Nancy commented.

"That's what makes the case so interesting," Chris remarked. "Obviously, there must be a very talented artisan involved in the scheme—"

"Or an agile assistant who substitutes the fake items for the real ones after the customers' bids are in," Nancy concluded.

"Very astute," Chris complimented her. "Maybe you ought to work with Ted."

"Except that he prefers to work alone," Jacqueline added.

"As it is," Nancy smiled pleasantly, "I already have my own mystery to solve."

The curiosity in the faces of her listeners encouraged the young detective to explain.

"You see, Mr. Reese, the designer, has asked me to help him find a thief."

"Really?" Jacqueline asked, throwing a quick glance at Chris.

"In fact," Nancy continued, "several gowns, which you were to have modeled last night, Jackie, disappeared from the hotel."

"How terrible!" Chris exclaimed. "Do you have any leads yet?"

"Nothing definite," Nancy said vaguely. She decided not to mention the stranger she had discovered in the dressing room.

"Forgive me for saying this," Chris went on, "but I think you ought to leave that sort of investigation up to someone with experience."

"Like Ted Henri?" Nancy replied, her mouth becoming a thin line.

"Nancy has had a lot of experience as a detective," Bess defended her friend.

"Oh, I'm sure she has," Chris answered. "It's just that you never know how tough things might get, and I wouldn't want anything to happen to her, or you, for that matter."

"Well, nothing has so far," George spoke up.

"Even so," Jacqueline commented, "Chris is right."

"And to think we were going to offer to look for your brother—undercover, of course," Nancy said quickly.

"We were?" George raised her eyes with uncertainty.

Jacqueline looked at Chris with an urgent, almost pleading expression and fidgeted with the handle of her bag.

"What do you think?" the model asked him.

"It's up to you," he sighed.

"We wouldn't do anything to mess up Ted's investigation," Bess put in.

"I imagine he's trying to gather as much evidence as he can against the auction house," Nancy said. "I'm sure he doesn't want police interference, so we'd have to keep a low profile."

"It's a good idea, isn't it, Chris?" Jacqueline pressed.

"Yes, so long as these young ladies think

they're able to handle it," the photographer replied. "Tell me, Nancy, how do you plan to start your search for Ted?"

Nancy was thoughtful for a moment, then smiled. "Well, first we have to find the lion's crest!"

6

Medallion Mystery

"I wonder what the lion's crest means," Bess said, pondering Ted Henri's message.

Nancy was thinking about the variety of architecture she had seen throughout the city, especially the pair of stone lions that flanked the entrance to the New York Public Library. Was it possible that a lion's crest existed somewhere on a building where Ted might be hiding out?

"How about the auction houses?" George put in. "Do any of them have a lion's crest on the canopy?"

"Not to my knowledge," Chris said, "but it's possible."

As he spoke, Bess picked up a thick telephone directory and began to scan the classified section.

"Look at all the auction houses!" she exclaimed in discouragement. "There must be a hundred of them!"

"Not quite that many," Nancy said, snatching a glance at the list.

"Even so," George said, "it will take more than a few days to visit all of them."

Nancy noticed a newspaper lying on a desk. "Chris, may I look at that?" she asked.

"Of course," he replied, sensing what was on her mind. "Maybe you'll find something under 'galleries.' I was just about to suggest it myself."

Nancy quickly located the page filled with announcements about various auctions. One in particular drew her attention.

"There's an interesting sale scheduled tonight at Speers, Limited," she pointed out, adding that among the items being auctioned off were heraldic shields and medallions. "Maybe we'll find something bearing a lion's crest among them!"

"And perhaps Ted!" Jacqueline added excitedly.

"It's a shame we missed the preview exhibition," Nancy said. "That was this morning. But if we try, we can make the auction at 8 P.M."

"By the way," George said to Jacqueline,

"what does your brother look like? In case he happens to be there, we'd like to tell you."

"Oh, well, he's taller than I am and he has dark wavy hair and hazel eyes. His face is rounder than mine. It's ruddier, too."

"Do you have a picture of him?" Bess asked.

"No, unfortunately—only a childhood photograph, and I assure you we both have changed a lot since then." The model laughed, tossing back her mane of hair, letting the lamplight pick up highlights.

Before the girls left, Bess whispered to Jackie out of earshot of her friends and then jotted something on a piece of paper.

"What's up?" George asked her cousin when they stood on the sidewalk again.

"You'll see," Bess replied, mysteriously. "I have to run now. See you back at the apartment. 'Bye."

Like a bolt of lightning, she flashed down the street and disappeared into a taxi that had stopped to let off a passenger.

Nancy and George gaped at each other, breaking into giggles as they realized that Bess's admiration for the glamorous model was probably at the root of her latest adventure. The afternoon passed quickly at Aunt Eloise's and when the doorbell finally rang, Nancy and

George ran to answer the door together!

"Bess, is that you?" Nancy asked, gaping at her friend, while George put a hand over her mouth, biting her lips to keep from laughing out loud.

Bess looked hurt. "What do you think? Of course, it's me!"

She had obviously gone to a hair and makeup artist who had changed everything except the color of her eyes. Her hair was swept upward in small fine ringlets, a few of which dangled over her ears and around the base of her neck.

"Well?" Bess said, noting that her friends had fallen into total silence.

"The hair isn't bad," George said, "but those eyes! Wow!"

Nancy, too, was spellbound by the transformation. False eyelashes, curled thickly over Bess's own, appeared to be half an inch long! One had loosened and Bess had carelessly stuck it back above the lid, making her look like a Paul Klee painting.

"Did Jacqueline recommend this?" Nancy inquired.

"Not *this*. Him," Bess said. "He's a wonderful hair stylist and makeup man. All the models go to him."

She marched to a mirror in the living room,

quickly observing the lopsided eyelash. Embarrassed, she hurried to adjust it, but it drooped down over the lower lid and came loose, leaving her with one set on and the other off.

George roared as Bess turned around. She grimaced angrily at her cousin.

"You're just jealous!" Bess charged.

"Jealous!" George laughed, and grabbed her camera which she had left on a small table in the foyer. "I can't miss this one. Dave will love it!"

"Don't you dare!" Bess cried, tearing off the other set of lashes.

But it was too late. Her cousin had already snapped a picture. "Here she is, folks. The new model of the year!" George said gleefully, taking the finished print out of the camera.

All through supper neither of the cousins spoke to each other, which made Nancy and her aunt feel uncomfortable.

"I like your hair, dear," Aunt Eloise complimented Bess, causing her to smile briefly.

"Thank you very much," she said. "Please pass the salt, Nancy."

That was the extent of Bess's conversation until they reached the auction house of Speers, Limited. They noticed that most of the audience were holding catalogs, and Nancy hurried to a desk to purchase one.

"Ooh, there are some gorgeous things in that book!" Bess said to the others, after glancing at someone else's brochure.

Nancy quickly leafed through hers, pausing now and then to look at stunning color photographs of Old English silver and Oriental porcelain.

"Go back a few pages," George said shortly.

Nancy did so and, to her amazement, discovered the entry of a medallion that bore the head of a lion! It had belonged to a man named Galen Kaiser.

Was this what Ted Henri was referring to in the mysterious message he sent to his sister?

The girl detectives were careful not to discuss their find openly. Instead, they scanned the audience, looking for someone who matched Ted's description. A couple of men came close to it, but one had a bulbous nose and the other a ring of pock marks under his eyes. Jackie had not mentioned either of those characteristics.

Then the auction started and the girls' attention was drawn to a number of fine gold teacups. They were displayed on a velvet table that swung into view on a moving platform.

"Shall we bid?" George asked teasingly as the auctioneer called out successive bids.

"I have five hundred dollars. Do I hear more?" he said.

"Well, I'm not really looking for gold tea-cups," Nancy responded lightly.

One after the other, items from the estates of several wealthy people passed in and out of sight. Nancy and the cousins eagerly awaited the medallion.

"Here it comes!" Bess murmured as it appeared on the table, glittering under the spotlight.

From where the young detectives sat, they could not see it fully. Then, the auctioneer covered the microphone with his hand and turned sideways to speak to his assistant, completely obscuring the table from the girls' view. When he addressed the audience again, the young detectives were surprised to see that the medallion was gone. A small gold dish with a stand-up rim stood in its place!

"Do you suppose the medallion was stolen?" Bess whispered to her friends, who did not reply.

The auctioneer soon announced that the order of entries had been changed and the medallion would go up for bid shortly.

"Maybe somebody is switching the real one for a fake," Bess continued.

"That would be too obvious," George declared.

When the medallion came into view again, Nancy leaned forward. She didn't want to miss anything that was about to happen!

The bidding started. One hundred, two hundred, up to five hundred dollars!

"It's only estimated at one hundred fifty," Nancy informed the cousins. She held up her hand, signaling an offer.

"Are you crazy?" Bess cried under her breath, as the auctioneer announced Nancy's bid of five hundred fifty.

"I'm just curious," the young detective replied, waiting for one of two other bidders to respond.

Both of them had seemed unusually eager to buy the piece, but now they were silent.

"Going once, twice," the auctioneer said slowly. He held his mallet ready to pound on a desk.

Panic-stricken, Nancy realized that she was about to become the proud owner of something she really didn't want. Not only that, she would have to drain her savings account to pay for it!

7

The Fake Bidder

The auctioneer held the mallet a moment longer, glancing at the men who had bid first on the medallion. Nancy's heart pounded as she prayed that one of them would raise his hand.

She didn't see the signal, but the auctioneer suddenly said, "Six hundred dollars. I have a bid of six hundred. Do I hear more?"

"Whew!" Bess exclaimed, echoing Nancy's own relief. "What would you have done?"

"I'd probably have to scrub Dad's office for the rest of my life!" Nancy said.

"Why did you bid on that thing, anyway?" George inquired.

Nancy shrugged. "I did it on the spur of the moment, thinking perhaps I'd get some reaction from those men by starting to compete with them."

Nancy paused a moment, then added, "And I was hoping that if I entered the bidding, I might pick up a clue as to why they both wanted the medallion."

"Well, it didn't happen," George said.

Nancy nodded. She wondered if the men would challenge each other further, but the medallion went to the one who had offered six hundred dollars.

Eagerly the girls watched the rest of the auction. A set of Meissen dinnerware was sold to a woman. Georgian candlesticks went to someone else and an unusual array of dinner bells to a third person. The men who had bid for the medallion remained silent throughout the balance of the sale.

When it was over, Nancy rose to her feet. "I'd like to congratulate the winner," she told her friends.

"We're sticking with you," Bess said, following her cousin and Nancy through the crowd.

The man who had bought the medallion was short, with a bald head that shone like a billiard ball, and Nancy was able to keep him in sight easily. He went to a counter already filled with winning bidders who wished to claim their prizes. When one woman stepped away with a small carton, he quickly took her place.

Nancy and her friends moved behind him, noticing the name stamped on the check he signed. It was Russell Kaiser!

Was he related to Galen Kaiser? the girls wondered. If so, why would he have bid on something that belonged to the Kaiser family in the first place?

"Mr. Kaiser," Nancy said as a clerk handed him the medallion, "I wanted to—"

"Aren't you the person who forced the bid to six hundred?" he grumbled.

"Yes, I am," Nancy replied, somewhat embarrassed.

"Humph."

"May I ask you a couple of questions?" she went on boldly.

"What about?"

"The medallion, of course."

"I'm sorry, miss. I have a dinner party to go too and I'm late already. Excuse me."

He brushed past her, muttering under his breath, and hurried toward an exit sign.

"He certainly wasn't very friendly," George said. "I wonder why that medallion is so important."

"I guess we'll never know," Bess commented with disappointment.

Just then a voice behind them stopped the conversation. "Miss Nancy Drew?" a man asked, causing the girls to face the other bidder on the medallion.

He was blond, about forty, and had thick, straight eyebrows that lay close together over a long and rather slim nose.

"I'm Nancy Drew," the young detective spoke up, surprised that he knew her name.

"I'm Russell Kaiser."

"Huh?" Bess replied, incredulous.

"No, *that* was—" Nancy started to say, quickly catching herself. She let the man continue.

"I recognized you from a newspaper article that covered a recent mystery you solved," he went on.

"Which one?" Nancy replied.

"I'm sorry to say I really don't remember," he said, blushing.

"Are you sure your name is Kaiser?" George asked, unable to restrain herself any longer.

"Of course."

"We don't mean to sound presumptuous," Bess said, "but the gentleman who just bought that medallion claimed *he* was Russell Kaiser."

"What? That's impossible."

"His name was on the check he signed."

Immediately, their listener pulled out a checkbook, then other identification cards, glancing through them rapidly.

"Everything's here," he said, slipping them back into his coat pocket. "But I've got to stop payment on that man's check in case he's trying to draw money out of my bank account!"

He hurried to the desk clerk, spoke to him briefly, then returned to the girls.

"Mr. Kaiser—" Nancy began.

"Call me Russell."

"Okay, Russell. If you don't mind my asking, I'd like to know why two men would bid three times the estimated value of that medallion."

Her listener hesitated a moment before speaking. "I just returned from a business trip and found a letter from an old friend of my uncle's," he began.

"Your uncle was Galen Kaiser?" Nancy inquired.

"Yes. His friend indicated that he wished to have the medallion for sentimental reasons. Everything, though, had been shipped to the auction house already, and there was no way to get hold of the medallion before the bidding started. So the only thing I could do was bid on it myself."

"What a shame," Bess commented, thinking

64

the man had not only lost out on the piece for his uncle's friend but an impostor had walked away with it!

"Are you sure your uncle's friend only wanted the medallion for sentimental reasons?" Nancy inquired.

Russell seemed puzzled by the question. "What do you mean?"

"Well," Nancy went on, "isn't it strange that someone else would have bid so much for the piece?"

"Nancy's right," Bess said. "There must be something about the medallion that none of us realizes."

"I certainly don't know what it is," he said. "I bid as much as I could possibly afford, but then—" His voice trailed off and he looked as if he were about to cry. "My uncle was a fine man—good to his friends, and they loved him. I happen to know that the man who wrote to me helped my uncle at a time when he needed it."

Although the girls knew nothing about the Kaiser family, they were overwhelmed by the nephew's obvious sensitivity. If only they could capture the stranger and rescue the medallion!

"Will you help me find the impostor?" the man pleaded.

"Definitely," Bess replied.

"I'll give a complete description of him to the police," Nancy volunteered and stood up to go to the nearest telephone.

"Wait!" Russell said. "I'd rather postpone that for the time being. You see, my family is well-known, and I'd like to avoid any publicity about this. If you don't track the man down on your own, we can call the police then."

Nancy hesitated a moment, but then acceded to the man's wishes. "We'll see what we can come up with," she promised. "Where can we reach you?"

"Here," he replied, handing her a printed card. "I work out of my home," he added.

The address, to Nancy's surprise, was not in a chic East Side neighborhood. It was in the heart of midtown, west of Fifth Avenue.

"We'll be in touch as soon as we have something to report," she said.

On the way back to Aunt Eloise's apartment, the girls discussed the strange events of the evening.

"It's really peculiar," George commented. "We go to an auction looking for Ted Henri and wind up hunting for Russell Kaiser's impersonator."

Nancy nodded thoughtfully. "I guess we've stumbled on a completely new mystery!"

8

A Precious Secret

The next morning, the girls were up early. "What's our program for today?" Bess asked when they all were seated around the breakfast table.

"I think we should go the police station and take a look at the mug shots. Perhaps we can find a lead to the identity of the fake Russell Kaiser," Nancy declared.

"Good idea," George declared.

"I also want to call Jackie, just to make sure that neither of the two men we saw last night was Ted."

As soon as Nancy swallowed her last mouthful of scrambled eggs, she contacted the model. Jacqueline confirmed that her brother did not have a bulbous nose or any pock marks under his eyes.

"I'm sorry you weren't successful," she added.

"Well, we've come upon another interesting mystery in the interim," Nancy said, and told the young woman about the medallion with the lion's head on top and the two Russell Kaisers. "I don't know if there's a connection between the symbol on your brother's note and the figure on the medallion, but we're following it all up. I am leaving for the police station now."

"My, you are a busy detective." The model laughed into the phone.

Nancy smiled. "My stockpile of mysteries is getting a little heavy," she admitted. "After we finish talking to the police, I'll have to stop by Mr. Reese's office."

"He happens to be near a wonderful little dress shop, which you all must see," Jackie said. "Promise me you'll go." She gave Nancy the address.

The girl detective chuckled, secretly wondering if the dresses would be as outlandish as the makeup results on Bess.

"We'll let you know if we buy anything," she concluded the conversation.

Bess and George had already slipped into their coats and waited impatiently for Nancy to put hers on. Then they said good-bye to Aunt

Eloise, who was also preparing to leave.

"Marjorie and I have to tally the proceeds of the show this morning," she informed her niece.

"Well, I hope you made a whole bucket full of money and—" Nancy said when the ring of the telephone interrupted her.

"You take it, dear," Aunt Eloise said.

To Nancy's surprise, it was a telegram from her father! She listened intently to the message which the operator read:

COULD NOT REACH YOU BY PHONE. SENDING IM-PORTANT PAPERS TODAY. PLEASE WAIT FOR THEM.

"How strange!" Nancy said to her friends as she hung up the receiver.

"Who was it?" Bess asked.

"Dad—I mean a telegram from Dad."

"That *is* odd," George remarked. "Of course, we came in late last night, but he could have called this morning. Maybe you ought to try phoning him."

The same thought had occurred to Nancy. She made two telephone calls, one to the house where Hannah told her that her father had al-ready left for the office, and the other to the office where his secretary informed her that Mr. Drew was off on an all-day business appointment.

"Well, I can't chance it," Nancy told the other girls. "If Dad wants me to wait for documents, I'd better do it."

She took off the coat that hung loosely on her shoulders and returned it to the closet.

"Of course, this doesn't mean you girls have to stick around," she added.

Bess and George looked at each other undecidedly. George finally suggested that they could save some time if she and Bess checked out the police mug shots.

"Good idea," Nancy concurred. "By the time you get back, I ought to have the papers, and then we can head for Mr. Reese's."

"Are you sure you don't mind?" Bess said, knowing that Nancy would have liked to review the police pictures herself.

"I'm positive," Nancy said. "You saw the same man I did at the auction."

That was reassurance enough to send the girls on their way.

"Oh, wait a minute," Nancy said. "Here, take this. It's the address of a dress shop Jacqueline told me about. Since we're running short on time, maybe you ought to stop there before you come back."

"Great!" Bess exclaimed.

Nancy handed each of the girls an umbrella from the closet. To Bess she said, "It's supposed to rain today. I'm sure you don't want those new curls to come undone." The tiny curls that had framed her face the day before had begun to sag a bit, but Bess was determined to keep the hairdo.

In reply, Bess merely rolled her eyes and said, "Be back soon."

Leaving Nancy to wait for the mysterious documents, Aunt Eloise followed the cousins out the door. When they arrived at the police station after a circuitous ride in a taxicab that had deposited Eloise Drew en route, George introduced herself and Bess.

"We're friends of Nancy Drew, the amateur detective."

The sergeant on duty had heard of Nancy and smiled. "Are you helping her on a case?" he inquired.

George nodded. "That's why we're here. We'd like to take a look at mug shots, if you don't mind. We're searching for a man whose name we don't know."

"What'd he do?" the sergeant asked.

"Impersonated a client of ours who doesn't want any publicity about it. We promised to try finding the man on our own."

"I see. Well, go ahead. Take a look at our file."

He led them into a room and provided the photographs they had requested.

"Thanks," the girls chorused almost in unison.

"Let me know if you recognize the guy!" The sergeant grinned.

For several minutes, the young detectives pored over the pictures, stopping once in a while to stare at a face that seemed familiar. A couple of the men bore similar features to the impostor—a bald head, for instance, but the shape of the eyes or nose was different.

"Hey!" Bess said suddenly as they reached the bottom of the pile. "Look at this!"

The girls stared at a photograph of a man in his late thirties, maybe early forties, whose eyes were pinched together under thick, straight brows. His nose was long and slim, the mouth full, and the face was framed by blondish hair.

"It's Russell Kaiser!" George gasped. "Not the bald man who bought the medallion and who we assumed to be the impostor. It's the man who approached Nancy and asked us to help him!"

"His real name is Pete Grover, and he's wanted for check forgery in the State of California," Bess added. "It says so right here under the picture."

"Maybe the sergeant has more information about him. Let's ask," George suggested.

The officer was very interested when he heard that they found a man in the mug shots who resembled someone they had met the night before.

"Now, you say you saw him at an auction," the sergeant asked. "Did he buy anything?"

"No," George replied, "but he bid on a medallion. He didn't get it, though."

The policeman nodded. "We'll look into it."

"What do you think is going on?" Bess asked her cousin on the way out.

"Beats me, but I have a hunch we'll have to do a little more investigating before we find out. Pete Grover's hair was a little different, but I'm sure he was the man we met last night."

The girls headed for the dress shop on East 67th Street. It was small and stocked with expensive, imported clothes.

"No wonder Jacqueline comes here," Bess commented. She thumbed through the hangers, pausing to look at a gold lamé jumpsuit. "These pants are meant for sticks to wear."

George laughed. "Well, that lets you out!"

"Very funny," said Bess, who was used to

73

being teased by George about her waistline. She shoved the suit along the rack. "Now, here's something. Oh, I want to try it on."

Before George could get a close look at what it was, Bess dashed into a dressing room in the back of the store. Within a few minutes, a clerk went after her, then returned to the rack for a larger size.

George sat down on a velvet cushion, preparing for Bess's entrance. She heard peculiar noises from the dressing room—sighs, and then giggles.

"Ready or not," Bess called out at last.

She stepped into view, watching the frozen look in her cousin's eyes.

"Like it?" she asked gaily.

George gulped.

The one-piece pants suit was a shimmer of silver and black that ballooned over Bess's figure, ending in a tight hug over her ankles. Bess turned in front of a mirror and grinned at George.

"Cat got your tongue?" she asked.

"Mm-hmm," George said. "You're a true vision."

"Thanks," Bess replied, evidently pleased. "How much is it?" she asked the clerk.

"Only four twenty-five."

"Four hundred and twenty-five dollars?" Bess gasped. "Oh, and I do love it!"

"Well, maybe you can find a dressmaker in River Heights to sew something like it," George consoled her.

"These are one of a kind," the clerk insisted haughtily.

"I'm sure," George replied. "Let's go."

"I'm so disappointed," Bess said when they were outside again.

"Just think of it this way. If you had bought that outfit, Dave would have thought something had happened to the good old Bess he once knew! Besides, it would have looked better on a thinner girl."

"Good old Bess. That's me," Bess sighed. "I guess I'm just never going to be very sophisticated."

When they reached the apartment again, they were still talking about their excursion. George described the silver-black creation Bess had wanted to purchase, then they discussed the visit to the police station. Nancy was flabbergasted when she heard about the photograph they had seen.

George mentioned something that had been on her mind. "If Pete Grover is the impostor, though, why would he have deliberately introduced himself to you?" she asked Nancy.

"I have no idea."

"What about the papers your father sent? Did they come?" Bess inquired.

"No. A few letters arrived for Aunt Eloise. That was all. But I figure Dad must've mailed everything by special delivery, which means it could turn up here almost any time today."

The girls prepared a light lunch, and when they were done, it was almost two o'clock.

"I really ought to go to Mr. Reese's office," Nancy decided.

"If you want us to wait here, we will," George offered.

"But suppose the papers come and Nancy has to do something with them right away?" Bess objected. "No, I think she'd better stick around."

"I agree," Nancy said, "but I'd hate to spend the entire day cooped up in Aunt Eloise's apartment waiting for something that might never arrive. Maybe Dad's secretary can tell me where he is. I don't like to disturb him during a business meeting, but what else can I do?"

She called the attorney's office once more and, to her delight, discovered that her father had returned earlier than expected.

"What's up, dear?" Carson Drew asked pleasantly.

"Did you send me a telegram today?"

"No."

"And some important papers?"

"Papers? Why, no!"

As quickly as she could, Nancy gave an account of recent events, ending with the mysterious message.

"It was a phony, Nancy," her father said gravely. "Someone obviously didn't want you to leave the apartment for a reason!"

9

Fashion Accusation

But who? And why would anyone play such a mean trick on me? Nancy wondered.

When Mr. Drew heard about the events at the fashion show, he sounded even grimmer. "It seems to me that someone thinks you're getting too close for comfort."

"Thanks for the compliment, Dad, but I don't feel very close to anything."

"Maybe you just can't see the forest for the trees," the lawyer said. "And before you get lost in the wilderness, I want you to promise to call me every day!"

"I will, Dad. And I won't get lost. You'll see."

His deep, reassuring voice was enough to bolster Nancy's confidence. "We have a lot to do," she told her friends. "I've been thinking about my conversation with Jacqueline this morning."

"And?" George prompted.

"And I wonder if she has passed information along to the fashion thief who figured he'd keep me from going to Reese Associates today."

"You think Jacqueline is an accomplice in some way?" Bess asked in disbelief.

"No, but she could be an innocent conduit."

Her listeners pondered the idea for a moment.

"She and Chris are the only people who know you're trying to help Mr. Reese," George said.

"Also, it was only moments after I talked to her that the telegram came," Nancy added.

"Maybe we ought to talk to her again," George suggested.

"She's probably working now," Bess said. "A model who's as popular as Jacqueline would be in great demand."

"I'd like to visit Mr. Reese first, anyway," Nancy stated. "I don't want to give away my schedule again—"

"Especially to a thief!" Bess interrupted.

When the girls arrived at the designer's office, Nancy was pleased to learn that he had returned from the business trip he had been on the day before, and was out doing some investigating on his own!

"Did he leave a message for me?" she asked the receptionist, whose long, polished fingernails sifted through a basket of papers on her desk. "I'm afraid I don't see anything marked for Nancy Drew," she said, lifting her head in a smile. "Perhaps you ought to speak with Mr. Reese directly. He's at Zanzibar's."

The name didn't sound familiar to the girls.

"It's a photographic studio," the receptionist went on. "They do a lot of catalog work for major department stores."

"Okay," Nancy said. "If by any chance Mr. Reese should return before we get there, will you tell him I'm looking for him?"

"Will do."

The receptionist jotted down the address of the studio, which was located in the heart of the garment district. The buildings were gray and, apart from a sign that said Zanzibar's, the young detectives might have passed by without realizing what it was. The entrance was small, too. There were a few color advertisements from old store catalogs that hung on the wall, but no evidence of what lay beyond.

Nancy led the way to a desk at the end of the hall, where a stubby woman was seated. She greeted the visitors pleasantly, but when Nancy mentioned the name Reese, the woman stiffened.

"He is talking with one of our photographers," she said, "and I'm sure they don't wish to be disturbed."

"But Nancy is trying to help him investigate the thefts from the hotel last night," Bess blurted out.

The woman stared at Nancy. "You hardly look like a detective," she said, as shouting voices broke through a far door.

Nancy recognized Mr. Reese's instantly. She strode past the receptionist with Bess and George close at her heels.

"You can't go in there!" the stubby woman cried, but the girls had already opened the door.

"My models are getting paid plenty by the hour," the photographer was barking at Mr. Reese, "and you're taking both *my* time and theirs!"

A young brunette, who was standing in front of a long sheet of seamless blue paper, moved out of the strong light that poured over her.

"It's getting too hot for me," the detectives overheard her remark. The men, however, had missed the comment.

"I am going to have you arrested, Mr. Vinton!" the fashion designer yelled.

"Fine! Go ahead!"

"Oh, Nancy, let's get out of here," Bess whispered.

"And that includes your assistant!" Reese was pointing a threatening finger at a woman in slacks and a smock who was standing near the model. He charged angrily toward her. "What's your name?" he growled, pushing aside one of the tall lights.

It teetered, then crashed to the floor in splinters of glass!

"Oh!" the woman cried as a chunk slid close to her foot. "You're a madman! That's what you are!"

Reese boiled at the remark. "You haven't seen anything yet!" he fired at her, shoving the young model out of the way and tearing the paper off a metal bar.

"Mr. Reese! Please, Mr. Reese!" Nancy called from the doorway.

But the man paid no attention. His face and neck were a blaze of red as he turned back to the photographer, who grabbed him firmly by the shoulders.

"I am going to throw you out personally!" Vinton roared.

"Stop him, somebody!" Bess trembled as

Reese swung a fist at the man, just missing him.

By now the noise had traveled through the whole studio, where, behind several closed doors, other photo sessions were being conducted. One after another, people infiltrated Mr. Vinton's room and, at last, two men tackled Reese before he could land another swing.

"I'll send you a bill for this mess!" Mr. Vinton rasped loudly.

"And I'll see to it that you pay for every dress you filched!" the designer snapped, as Nancy stepped closer to interrupt.

"Mr. Reese," she said firmly, catching his attention at last.

"What do you want?" he grumbled.

"You should be careful about making accusations you can't back up."

Now the man laughed hard. He flexed his arms, seeking to be free of the tightening hold.

"That's very funny. Are you a lawyer, too?"

Nancy took a deep breath and Bess and George pulled behind her.

"No, I'm not a lawyer," the girl replied calmly. "But I do know that you can get into an awful lot of trouble if you can't support your charges."

"Well, I can support them," he snarled. "These men are nothing more than cheap crooks, and if I ever find out who commissioned them to photograph my clothes, I will sue them!"

The girls wondered if Zanzibar's had, in fact, photographed the copies of Mr. Reese's original designs that had appeared in the Millington catalog. Nancy noticed the torn page of one sticking out of his coat pocket.

"Is that from the Millington book?" she asked.

"No. This is from the Chalmers catalog," the designer replied, referring to an expensive department store.

He whipped out the page and waved it under Nancy's nose, his hand still trembling in rage. "Here, look for yourself. See these two gowns? High-priced merchandise, wouldn't you say? Not at all like the stuff Millington manufactures. But they're my designs, too!"

"What makes you think the photographer had something to do with the theft?" Nancy inquired.

"Because he wouldn't tell me who gave him the assignment! He's covering up for someone, I'm sure of it!"

10

A New Discovery

Nancy stared at the pictures in the Chalmers catalog. The two beautiful gowns Reese had indicated were, in fact, credited to Arnaud Hans, a competing designer!

The girl's mind was racing with questions, but she decided to wait until they had left the studio before asking them.

"I think we should go," she said to Mr. Reese. "There's nothing more we can accomplish here."

Apparently the temperamental designer agreed, because he walked to the door. "You'll hear from my lawyer!" he called back to Vinton.

"And you from *ours*!" the photographer replied coldly as the girls followed Reese out the door.

The young detectives trooped after him to his office past the receptionist and into an oak-paneled room where he gestured for them to sit.

"Mr. Reese, who saw your spring collection before all of these terrible things began to happen to you?" Nancy asked.

"Very few people," he replied.

"Would you mind giving me their names?"

"Chris Chavez is one."

"Chris Chavez, the photographer?" Nancy was aghast. "I thought a collection wasn't supposed to be photographed before it was shown in public."

"Well, Chris didn't shoot anything, but he's a good friend, and I showed him a few things."

"Who else had access to the designs?" George inquired.

"Only three, maybe four other people on my staff, and they're all trustworthy. Now, if you will excuse me, I have some important appointments."

He led the girls to the door, indicating that he didn't wish to continue the discussion.

"I think he was insulted when you asked him about the people he had shown his collection to," George said to Nancy on the way out.

"I think he's just upset about everything that happened," Bess declared.

"Well, he isn't helping his own case very much," Nancy remarked, "which means we'll have to put on two thinking caps apiece!"

"I can easily wear two, but I doubt that Bess can!" George laughed. She eyed the mountain of curls her cousin had coaxed back into place after trying on clothes that morning.

Bess tugged on a few stray wisps, saying, "I'm going to pretend you never said that, George Fayne."

Another round of teasing was brewing, which Nancy decided to cut short. "I have a choice," she said.

"A choice?" Bess replied.

"Yes, I can either try to get a job with the Millington Company or with Chalmers."

"Are you kidding?" George said. "You've never worked for anybody in your whole life—other than your father, of course."

"I know," Nancy said, "but there's always a first time. Besides, how else am I going to get any inside information?"

The cousins had to admit Nancy was making good sense.

"Can you type?" Bess asked.

"Some."

"Take shorthand?" George inquired.

Nancy shook her head. "But I can scrub floors

if I have to." She giggled. "What about you?"

"You mean we have to get jobs also?" Bess asked.

"Well, I won't be able to work in two places at the same time," Nancy persisted.

"Okay, okay," Bess said. "I'll sure try. But how about a snack first? I'm starved!"

The girls went into a nearby restaurant where Nancy found a Manhattan telephone directory on a back table. She quickly located addresses for Millington and Chalmers, noted them on a pad, then headed into the dining room where Bess and George were already seated behind menus.

"Lunch was only three hours ago," Nancy said.

"So we'll have some dessert," Bess remarked. "I can't work on an empty stomach."

"That's assuming we get jobs," George said. "What if we don't?"

"And what if no one will interview us?" Bess added.

"Then I'd like you to track down Jacqueline and find out whom she may have talked to about the Reese investigation."

The cousins agreed and Bess shut her menu as if she had reached a decision.

"On second thought," she sighed, "I've been

thinking about that gorgeous silver and black pants suit. If I lose a few pounds—"

"And find four hundred and twenty-five dollars," George put in.

"I might be able to get into a smaller size and buy it when it goes on sale," Bess finished.

"By that time," Nancy said, "the suit will be out of style. Come on, let's go."

She rose to lead the way past the cashier when someone opened the restaurant door and held it for a woman in a wheelchair.

Through the open door, Nancy heard a man in the street greet another. "Well, if it isn't Chris Chavez. How've you been, buddy?"

"Oh, just fine, Sam," the other man replied. "Sorry I can't stop to talk to you, but I'm in a hurry."

Nancy stared at him in surprise. He had a short, sculpted haircut, and a pencil-thin mustache. Certainly he was not the photographer she had met!

The man waved to his friend and hailed a taxi. The door, meanwhile, was still blocked by the wheelchair and the girls had to wait. Nancy bit her lip, hoping she would get out in time to talk to the man. Was he really Chris Chavez? And if so, who was the man who had pretended to be the photographer?

Bess and George had witnessed the conversation, too, and now George tugged on Nancy's arm. "Do you believe this!" she whispered. "Now there are two impostors in our case!"

Nancy nodded. "I wish I knew how to solve this dilemma," she murmured, "or rather this *twin dilemma!*"

Finally the woman in the wheelchair was through the door. The girls rushed outside, but at the same moment, Chavez climbed into a cab that had pulled to the curb. Before the girls could reach him, however, the taxi pulled away!

"What are we going to do now?" Bess wailed.

"Proceed with our original plan," Nancy said. "Let's flip a coin. Heads, you take Chalmers, tails, I do."

A moment later, while Nancy went off by herself to tackle the Millington Company, Bess and George caught a bus to the Chalmers building. When the cousins reached it, they couldn't help comparing the lobby with that of the Zanzibar studio. Catalog covers in beautiful, gilt-edge frames hung low over spotlights, and the walls were papered in rich, brown suede that created an aura of luxury.

"I'm nervous," Bess admitted as she and George went to the personnel office.

An attractive woman wearing gold-rimmed

eyeglasses greeted them with a smile. "Are you applying for the secretarial jobs?" she asked.

"Were they the ones advertised in the paper?" George replied with an air of confidence.

"Yes."

"Then those are the ones we're interested in," George said, causing Bess to gulp.

"Fine. Please follow me, if you will," the woman responded.

She motioned them toward a table and asked them to fill out applications. Then, with only a brief glance at the forms, led them toward a room with a desk and typewriter.

"I have some material for you to type," she said. "I can see from your applications that you don't have much prior experience."

"None," Bess murmured to herself.

"Even so, I don't mind giving young talent a chance," the interviewer went on. "If you pass this test, we'll move on to the next one."

Next one! The cousins moaned. How many hurdles would they have to overcome before the company would hire them?

"Now, who wants to go first?" the woman inquired.

George offered instantly, but the confidence she exuded was short-lived as she stared at a mass of information she was instructed to type in orderly fashion.

"I'll shut the door," the woman told her, "so no one will disturb you."

For a moment, George froze in front of the typewriter. Then she set her fingers on the keys, pressing out a few words slowly and carefully until she was able to pick up speed. But as the words fell on the paper in rapid succession, she stopped paying close attention. It wasn't until she had finished one page of work that she realized what she had done! By mistake, she had typed most of it in capital letters and put in wrong punctuation!

"Oh, no!" She gasped in horror. "I've ruined it!"

She tore out the paper, slipping another one in place, racing to make up for lost time. But the keys jammed.

"It's no use!" George cried aloud, as the door opened.

"How are you doing?" the personnel manager inquired pleasantly.

"I'm not doing well at all," the girl admitted, pushing back her chair.

"You're not giving up, are you?"

George never liked being called a quitter, but she realized that she wasn't qualified for a secretarial job. Neither was Bess, who, meanwhile, had looked at magazines, including the current Chalmers catalog.

Remembering the page Mr. Reese had taken from another copy, she hunted for it and again studied the lovely gowns. When she saw the personnel manager coming out of the room with George, she had a sudden inspiration.

"These pictures are just beautiful," she said to the woman. "Do you know who photographed those gowns?"

The woman looked at the catalog. "Most of this collection, including those dresses, were done by Chris Chavez," she responded. "Doesn't he have a terrific flair?"

Bess nodded. She was as flabbergasted as George. Was Chris Chavez, Mr. Reese's personal friend, an accomplice to the thefts?

11

Puzzling Information

Meanwhile, Nancy had filled out an application at Millington. When the manager, whose name according to a sign on his desk was T. Iannone, reviewed it, he looked at her closely.

"So you want a job, eh? I think, Miss Drew, it's more likely you're here to snoop!"

His biting remark hit Nancy unexpectedly, and she decided to tell him the truth. "Could we speak privately?" she suggested, glancing at a nearby secretary who was pretending not to listen, but Nancy could see she was interested in the conversation.

"This way," the manager said, leading Nancy into an inner office. "I happen to know that you were Jacqueline Henri's replacement in the fashion show the other night—and that Richard

Reese has asked you to help track down a dress thief. News travels fast in this business."

"Yes, I can see that." The girl detective knew it wouldn't help to disguise her motive for being at Millington's and went straight to the point. "How do you explain the fact that copies of Mr. Reese's original dresses turned up in your spring catalog before the originals were made public?" Nancy asked.

"I have no idea."

"But you admit the Millington dresses are copies of Mr. Reese's," the girl reiterated.

"I'm not admitting anything. We run a very clean business here. Anyway, the Reese name doesn't appear with any of our merchandise, so obviously we're not making extra money off it."

That was an interesting clue, Nancy thought. Without the name of the designer attached to the clothes, they wouldn't be so valuable. So perhaps the thief cared less about the designs themselves and more about destroying Mr. Reese's business!

"Mr. Reese is very upset," the girl continued. "He's determined to get to the bottom of this and to sue whoever is involved in the matter."

The man yielded reluctantly. "What do you want me to do about it?" he asked.

"I want you to hire me so I can get to know a

few of the people who work around here."

Again there was a long pause.

"Tell me what kind of work you're capable of doing," Mr. Iannone sighed.

As he spoke, Nancy was aware of someone eavesdropping outside the door, but the person moved away upon realizing the manager was in conference.

"I'll gladly take any job that will provide contact with your staff."

"In that case, I suggest you help out as a stylist," he said, "You can begin tomorrow. In the meantime, I'll introduce you to someone who'll show you what to do."

He led the girl to a windowless workroom filled with a large table, dressing mirrors, an ironing board, and racks on which hung dresses with tags. In one corner stood a small desk.

"Now wait here," the manager said, closing the door.

"Thank you," Nancy said.

She peeked at the dresses, which were made of a rough cotton material, and noted the uneven stitching along the seams. Unlike the apparel in the Chalmers book, these clothes were cheap-looking.

Nancy went to a chair at the far end of the room and sat down. Suddenly, the lights went out, throwing her into total darkness!

A moment later, she heard shouts in the hallway. Doors were slamming, people were yelling, and it seemed to Nancy that a general panic had broken out.

The electricity must have gone off in all the offices, the girl said to herself. I'd better get out of here!

She groped her way through the room, careful to avoid the clothing racks, but then grazed against the corner of the table.

"Ouch!" Nancy winced and rubbed her hip. "That hurt!" From then on, she hesitated before every step. Finally, she made it to the door and fumbled for the knob. When she turned it, a flash of fear stabbed through her. The door was locked!

The young detective paused a moment, her mind whirling. Did someone lock her in on purpose? Mr. Iannone, perhaps? It must have happened after the lights went out, when all the noise started, she reasoned. Otherwise, she would have heard the click.

Who else knew I was in here? Did Mr. Iannone tell the person who was to train me? Nancy asked herself.

She banged her fist against the door and called out, but no one came.

Bess, in the meantime, was struggling through her own typing test. She went along more slowly than George, careful not to make any mistakes. But she had finished only half the assignment when the personnel manager stopped her.

"Time's up, dear," she said. "Now let me see what you've done."

Her smile faded rapidly when she realized that Bess had filled less than a page.

"It's very neat," she said, "but you'll have to build up your speed if you want to work here."

"Yes, ma'am," Bess replied, adding hopefully, "Is there something else I could try?" George had raised the same question.

"I don't think so," the woman said. "Let me check my files, though."

She disappeared briefly, letting the girls chat during her absence. Bess quickly told George that Chris Chavez had done the photos for the store catalog.

Soon the personnel manager returned with a folder. "Have either of you had any bookkeeping experience?" she asked.

"Not a bit," Bess said promptly.

"Well, I'm sorry, but I've nothing for you."

Before the cousins left, however, George decided to ask about Chris Chavez. "We met him at a benefit fashion show the other evening," she explained.

"Here in New York?" the woman replied in bewilderment. "Are you sure it was Chris?"

"Yes, why?"

"Because he's been on assignments for us in Europe. He only flew back to New York yesterday!"

The girls were surprised, but did not press the conversation further. Their job applications had just been turned down and they didn't wish to create undue suspicion about themselves. So, after thanking the woman for her evident kindness to them, they said good-bye and headed for Jacqueline Henri's apartment.

"Too bad we didn't get jobs at Chalmers," George said.

"I feel terrible," her cousin mumbled as their cab came to a halt in front of a building marked "15."

"Well, don't. Look at it this way," George said. "We picked up that great piece of information about Chris Chavez."

"Doesn't prove anything."

"Even so, it adds another intriguing aspect."

The girls stopped speaking as they opened the door of the apartment building. To their right was a bank of mailboxes and a small television screen. Ahead was another door that was locked.

"They sure believe in security, don't they?" Bess commented, pressing a button next to the name Henri.

A few minutes passed. Nothing happened and the girls concluded that the model was not at home.

"Let me try again," Bess said. This time she held the buzzer half a second more and a voice responded.

"Who is it?" The voice was distorted by the loudspeaker.

"Jacqueline, is that you?" Bess replied.

"Who?"

"I'm looking for Jacqueline Henri," Bess continued.

"There's no one here by that name," the voice said and clicked off.

George rechecked the address. It was correct! They scanned the names on the wall directory, discovering there was only one Henri listed.

"Maybe there's something wrong with the buzzer system," Bess said.

George tended to doubt that, but she was determined not to leave the building without visiting 3-C. As a couple came out through the locked doors, she quickly stepped up and held them open for Bess.

They rode the elevator to the third floor and turned left around a corner. There were no names on the apartment doors, only brass knockers. George was about to lift the one on 3-C when they heard a man's voice filter through.

"It's your job to keep Nancy occupied," he said, as he was walking toward the door.

"He's leaving!" George whispered. "Let's get out of here!"

Quickly, the girls scooted back toward the elevator. They heard the apartment door slam, and Bess grabbed George's hand. "He'll see us once he comes around the corner. What'll we do?"

"Let's hide on the other side," George gasped, and pulled her cousin in the opposite direction from apartment 3-C. They rounded another corner and pressed themselves closely against the wall.

The man's footsteps could be heard approaching the elevator. "I'm going to take a look," George declared boldly, and, for a second, she stuck her head around the corner. Then she pulled back with a little gasp, covering her mouth at the same time to stifle the sound.

Bess tugged impatiently on her cousin's hand. "Well, who is it?"

"Chris Chavez!"

"The first one or the second one?"

"The first one!"

They heard the elevator doors open. The man entered, and soon all was quiet as the elevator descended.

"Oh, I wish we could follow him!" Bess murmured.

"We can. Come on, down the stairs!"

George led the way to the stairwell. The girls flew down, taking two steps at a time, hoping the elevator would stop on another floor to delay Chavez. However, when they reached the lobby, the elevator was there, empty, and there was no sign of the photographer. Quickly, the young detectives hurried out into the street and looked in both directions. Nothing!

12

The Culprit

"We lost him!" George exclaimed angrily between gasps for air.

Bess shrugged. "Well, we tried. Let's go back to Aunt Eloise's and tell Nancy about this."

George nodded. "There's a bus pulling up on the corner. We'll have to run to catch it."

Bess groaned. "I'll never make it! I'm out of breath as it is!"

But George wasn't listening. She was already running toward the bus, with Bess trailing behind. They just managed to squeeze through the door before it closed.

"How do you know this is the right bus?" Bess panted.

"I don't, but let's hope so."

To the girls' chagrin, however, they soon discovered that they were heading away from Aunt Eloise's apartment. It was getting dark, too, and a damp chill had seeped into the bus.

"We'll get off the next stop," George said, but it proved to be a desolate corner, causing the two passengers to debark at the following one which seemed livelier.

There they caught a taxi and were home in less than fifteen minutes. Surprisingly, they discovered that Nancy had not yet returned.

"Where is she?" Aunt Eloise questioned when she saw that her niece wasn't with Bess and George. "She ought not to wander around the city alone at night."

Bess explained how they had tossed a coin which had sent Nancy to the Millington Company.

"Well, I'm sure they're closed now," Aunt Eloise said fearfully. "George, will you call their number?"

George complied at once, but there was no answer.

"The switchboard operator must have gone home," she said.

"Did you dial the right number?" Bess asked, observing the worrisome look on Eloise Drew's face.

"Of course, I did," the girl said. She dialed

again, however, to satisfy everyone, and again all she heard was a steady ring.

Nancy had been beating her fists on the workroom door in the Millington office, hoping someone would come to free her. But in the general confusion outside, no one seemed to hear. After a while, the shouts and footsteps died down as the office emptied out, and Nancy was left in the room all alone.

She stumbled through the darkness, bruising herself on the leg of an ironing board as she searched for the desk.

I have to find something flat, a letter opener perhaps, that I can use to force the lock! she said to herself.

She opened a side drawer and her fingers ran over pencils and paper clips before coming to rest on a slim cardboard box that contained filing tabs of some sort. Nancy took one, then went back to the door, shoving the tough sliver into the crack between the door panel and the frame. She pushed it down slowly, trying to slide it over the tumbler. But it jammed. Desperately she tried again. This time, the lock slipped and released.

Dropping the tab, Nancy opened the door

and felt her way into the adjoining stock room, where she groped for a light switch. She found one finally and pushed it, but nothing happened. Through the window she noticed that lights were on in the surrounding buildings. Their glow filtered dimly through the dusty glass.

Apparently, the blackout is restricted to this building, Nancy thought. Well, I'd better call Aunt Eloise.

She made her way slowly to the main office, letting her hands trail over a desk top until they settled on a telephone. To her dismay, however, she couldn't make a connection. All calls were apparently controlled by a switchboard that was closed.

Trying to remain calm, Nancy headed for the door that led to the reception area. To her relief, it was open!

The elevator is right across the hall from here, she thought. I hope it works!

When her outstretched hands made contact with the metal doors after she had crossed the corridor, she fumbled for the button and punched it. A slight hum indicated that the elevator was indeed operating!

"Thank goodness," the girl detective murmured, and stepped inside the car.

When she arrived on the ground floor, she found the main entrance unlocked. Instantly, she rushed outside to hail a taxi. The driver gabbed cheerfully, trying to engage her in conversation, but Nancy felt so tired all of a sudden she could only raise enough energy to suppress a series of yawns. By the time she reached the apartment, she was ready to fall asleep.

"Nancy!" Aunt Eloise cried upon seeing her. "Where have you been?"

The torrent of questions that followed from Bess and George woke the girl up immediately.

"We were just about to call the police!" George exclaimed.

"Oh, I'm glad you didn't," Nancy said, dropping into a chair.

She spun out her story as fast as she could, then listened to the others. Bess and George had made phenomenal discoveries, she told them.

"So it seems that the guy we saw in the restaurant today is the real Chris Chavez," Bess said.

"And the one who introduced himself to me at the party is someone else," Nancy put in. "Just who is he?"

"Well, we know he's a friend of Jacqueline's and he knows her brother," George commented.

"If I'd never heard about Ted Henri, investigative reporter," Nancy said, "I'd wonder if he weren't a figment of her imagination."

"Maybe Jacqueline's involved in the design thefts and when she heard you were coming to town, figured she had to cover up somehow," Bess suggested.

"But taking off the way she did before the fashion show and leaving Aunt Eloise in the lurch only drew attention to herself," Nancy replied.

"That's for sure," George said. "It made everybody suspicious."

"Us in particular," Bess concurred. She grappled with her bewilderment. "Jackie's behavior doesn't make any sense at all."

"Precisely," Nancy responded, "and I'm too tired to worry about it tonight. Let's try to figure out things tomorrow."

Before going to bed, however, Aunt Eloise spoke to Nancy alone.

"What are you going to do about that job you supposedly have at Millington?"

"Oh, I'm going back there tomorrow morning."

"After all that's happened to you? I don't

think it's a good idea," Aunt Eloise objected. "Of course, you realize you were locked in that workroom on purpose."

Nancy nodded. "But I want to find out who did it and why!"

Aunt Eloise still looked doubtful. "At least promise me you'll discuss it with your father first."

"I'll call Dad in the morning. And please don't worry, Aunt Eloise."

In spite of her exhaustion, the young detective slept fitfully that night. When she awoke the next morning, her eyelids were puffy and she had trouble keeping them open.

"Didn't you sleep?" George asked Nancy.

"Not very well." She yawned.

"This will wake you up," Bess said, putting a glass of grapefruit juice and the morning newspaper in front of her.

Nancy sipped the juice, allowing her eyes to fall on a small headline. Bess and George watched them pop.

According to the newspaper, Russell Kaiser's co-op apartment had been burglarized the night before! No mention was made about the nature of missing items, but Nancy wondered about the medallion. Had it been stolen and was there a connection between Kaiser's impostor and the robbery?

"I'd say it's a good thing we came along on this visit," George said. "Otherwise, Nancy, you'd be working forty-eight hours a day on these mysteries!"

Nancy laughed, dropping a piece of bread in the toaster. "You're absolutely right," she said, "and I have a hunch I'm going to need lots of energy again today!"

"Are you heading back to Millington?" Bess inquired.

"Definitely. I want to see Mr. Iannone first thing."

"What should we do?" George asked.

"How about visiting Russell Kaiser?" Nancy said.

"Which one?" Bess giggled.

"That's for you to figure out. Maybe you ought to stop by the apartment mentioned in this article."

Aunt Eloise, who had slept later than usual, stood in the doorway. Her presence reminded Nancy of their conversation the night before, and she quickly telephoned her father. Mr. Drew agreed that she should go back to Millington, but warned her to be careful.

"I will be," she promised, then invited Bess and George to meet her for lunch near the Millington office. "That way we can keep check on each other," Nancy said, raising a smile from her aunt.

Half an hour later, she was at Millington's reception desk. When she asked for Mr. Iannone, however, she was told he wasn't in.

"But he hired me yesterday," Nancy said to the receptionist.

Out of the corner of her eye, she noticed a brown-haired woman pass hurriedly through a door. Nancy turned her head, catching the face before she disappeared. The young detective was positive that it was Rosalind, the stylist whom Mr. Reese had hastily fired the night of the fashion show!

The girl at the desk now pressed a buzzer, calling someone to come out for a moment.

Soon, an officious woman in a green wool suit appeared. "This is Nancy Drew," the receptionist introduced the visitor.

Again Nancy asked for Mr. Iannone.

"He doesn't work here any longer," the woman informed her. "He quit yesterday."

Nancy gulped. "Quit!"

"Yes. Are you a personal friend of his, may I ask?"

"No, but he offered me a job here."

"Well, he had no authority to do so. I'm in charge now."

The steely tone in the woman's voice told the girl it would be tough to persuade her to go along with Mr. Iannone's decision. So Nancy took a different tack. She related her unpleasant experience in the workroom and her suspicions that it was somehow connected to the recent thefts from the Reese collection.

"My, you do have an active imagination," the woman said. "I'm quite positive that your trouble yesterday was an accident. I'm sorry about it, but I'm not going to hire you because of it!"

There was nothing left to say, so Nancy departed. Disappointed, she took the elevator to the lobby, not paying much attention to anyone until her eyes settled on the revolving doors ahead of her, and the man approaching them.

He looked familiar, but his head was bent low in a long, plaid scarf wrapped thickly around his neck. Nancy ducked into a magazine booth as he came forward, then watched as he loosened his scarf while he waited for an elevator.

Nancy had picked up a magazine, burying her face in it until she heard the door slide open. Then, as the stranger and several other people stepped inside, and turned to face the corridor, the girl lifted her eyes. The man was Jacqueline's friend who claimed to be Chris Chavez!

She dived back out of sight as the door hung open an extra second for a last-minute passenger. Then it closed and Nancy watched the bank of numbered lights as the elevator moved up slowly. It made two stops, one of which was Millington's floor!

If the man wasn't the real fashion photographer, what was he doing there? Was he the thief who had stolen the designs?

13

Baffling Trail

While Nancy's discovery had stunned her momentarily, Bess and George were preparing themselves for their own investigation.

"It's a good thing that the two impostors believe they've duped us totally!" Bess told her cousin.

"And we have to make sure they don't find out anything to the contrary," George said.

When the girls arrived at the apartment listed for Russell Kaiser in the news article, the doorman said he had strict instructions not to admit anyone while the police were still there.

"Have they been here a long time already?" George inquired.

The doorman glanced at his watch. "About thirty minutes," he said, "but they could be around the whole day, for all I know."

"Let's go," George said, and pulled Bess out the door.

"Where are we going?" her cousin inquired.

"Some place where we can stake out the building," George suggested.

The girls headed across the street toward a small coffee shop. Bess giggled. "If I have to stake out anything, there's no place I'd rather do it from than a coffee shop!"

"I bet," George answered. She carefully avoided patches of ice forming on the sidewalk and tried to scrape the icy granules that drizzled relentlessly out of the sky onto her coat sleeve. "This weather is terrible," she complained. "How can we investigate efficiently if we have to slip and slide everywhere we go?"

"Don't worry, we might have to sit here all day," Bess said, as they entered the restaurant.

George shook her head. "I wonder if Mr. Kaiser is even home. I think I'll call the apartment to see what I can find out."

She left Bess in a booth by the window and returned a few minutes later in a flurry of excitement. "The maid answered," George said. "Mr. Kaiser is leaving right now."

The girls dropped coins on the counter and dashed outside. The sidewalk was treacherous, slowing them to a snail's pace. Bess crept close to the shops, looking for iceless patches.

"Hurry!" George called back as she cut across the street.

Bess tried to, but felt the soles of her leather shoes skid forward. "You go ahead!" she cried.

The traffic light changed and she halted, watching George almost slide into the corner of Kaiser's apartment house.

She managed not to fall, however, and walked to the entrance where a bald-headed man was stepping into a patrol car that was parked in front.

He's the one who bought the medallion! she almost blurted.

Bess caught up to her as the car door closed, and George turned to her cousin excitedly. "That clinches it!" she exclaimed. "The second Russell Kaiser who asked Nancy to help is definitely the impostor! And even though his hair is different from that of the man we saw in the police picture, I'm sure he's Pete Grover!"

"He was bidding on that medallion like crazy," Bess said. "He must've really wanted it."

"But if he's a crook, why did he introduce himself to us?" George asked.

Bess had no answer, and no matter how much

they talked about the odd twists in the growing mystery, nothing satisfied them.

Nancy, at the same time, had gone into the restaurant across the street from the Millington office. It was still too early to expect Bess and George, Nancy realized, but she waited, wondering if Jacqueline's friend, whom she had spotted in the elevator, would come out again.

Traffic dragged on the ice-covered street, and a bus now blocked the girl's view of the revolving doors.

What if I miss him? Nancy worried, as the bus inched away.

She pressed closer to the window to look down the sidewalk, but saw no one who resembled the phony Chris Chavez. Minutes went by slowly, it seemed, but suddenly the man appeared! He paused outside the building and turned his head in both directions, apparently looking for someone.

I wonder if it's Jacqueline, Nancy thought. Just then, another bus pulled up right in front of her.

Oh, please move! she begged silently. I can't lose him now!

The vehicle moved along shortly and, to Nancy's relief, the man in the plaid scarf was still there talking to another man. Nancy gasped as she recognized him.

"That's Grover, the guy who told me he was Russell Kaiser," she said under her breath. "Where are they going?"

Figuring that Bess and George might be delayed by the bad weather, she decided to leave a message for them with the restaurant hostess and follow the two men.

"Please ask my friends to wait for me," Nancy told the young woman. Then she pulled up her coat collar and stepped cautiously onto the frozen sidewalk. She followed the men around the block, where they hurried into a fabric shop called Belini's, which boasted a variety of materials and sewing goods.

Through the window, the girl detective saw the men descend a flight of steps in the rear. She entered the store, taking quick note of the colorful polyester and cotton fabrics that were shelved in bolts.

A sign in the back indicated that the sewing supplies and offices were downstairs. Nancy followed the arrow, glancing down at the customers as she went below. The men were not in sight. Apparently, they had stepped into the office.

Nancy headed for a table with large pattern

books on it. She leafed through one, glancing up periodically to look for the two impostors.

"Excuse me, please," a woman said suddenly. Nancy had not been aware of the customer standing next to her, eager to look at the pattern book she was holding. "Are you finished with that?"

"Oh, yes," the girl replied as men's voices suddenly drifted over the sound of file drawers opening and closing.

The office, Nancy soon discovered, was located around a bend in the wall. Next to it was a tall column of narrow metal cabinets that contained all kinds of buttons. Without seeming too obvious, the girl secreted herself behind them. Now she was within better hearing range of the conversation.

"Mr. Belini," Nancy overheard Jacqueline's friend say, "I have only a few questions."

The young detective leaned forward eagerly, but someone approached the cabinets and opened a drawer, digging noisily through the buttons. Nancy quickly busied herself with swatches of material that hung behind her. Then, when the metal drawer slammed shut, she took her place again.

This time the other man was talking, and it seemed to Nancy that she heard the name

Rosalind. But his voice fell away in a drone of unintelligible words.

It's so frustrating, Nancy said to herself. She was tempted to leave her hiding place and move closer to the doorway, but what if she were caught? I can't take the chance, she decided.

She rested her hands on the stack of metal and dipped her head to one side. The pressure of her grip pitched the fragile cabinet forward and several drawers slid open, emitting hundreds of buttons!

They poured out in a steady stream despite the girl's attempt to right the cabinet quickly. Then her fingers slipped, and the whole structure crashed to the floor!

14

A Developing Pattern

As hundreds of buttons swirled out, Nancy hurried to the other side of the wall. She felt a lump harden in her throat as the three men ran out of the office.

"Again someone knocked over this cabinet," Belini complained. "Why don't people watch where they're walking?"

Two assistants seemed to appear from nowhere. "That whole setup is just terrible," one said. "We'll have to get a different type of cabinet. This one is so wobbly it falls at least once a week!"

While Belini mumbled something, they scooped up the buttons, separating them into their respective drawers. The three men, meanwhile, went back into Belini's office.

When the clerks finished with the cabinet, they hurried upstairs, allowing Nancy to position herself behind it once more. This time she carefully avoided touching it.

"How well do you know Mrs. Jenner?" she heard the phony Chris Chavez ask.

Belini said something in reply, which Nancy could not understand. Then his voice rose as he added, "Mrs. Jenner has a reputation for being abrasive. But she was a good worker, Mr. Henri, the best stylist around!"

Henri! Nancy couldn't believe her ears. Could it be that the phony Chris Chavez was really the reporter, Ted Henri?

A jumble of thoughts raced through the girl's mind. Why all the pretense? she wondered. And what was Ted Henri's affiliation with the phony Russell Kaiser, alias Pete Grover?

Was Henri investigating the same design thefts that Nancy was? Did they relate at all to the fake auction scheme he, as Chris Chavez, had revealed to Nancy?

Or maybe he trumped up the auction story for my benefit, hoping to sidetrack me onto another mystery! Nancy concluded.

As she continued listening, more questions came from the two men. They wanted to know what Belini's association with Millington was!

The young detective missed hearing Belini's answer as several customers entered the room from the stairway. They were chattering about a choice of colors, but then paused long enough for the girl to hear a few more remarks pass between the men.

"Do you supply fabric to Millington?" Henri questioned.

Belini grumbled something unintelligible.

Then Nancy heard Henri ask if Belini had sold material to Mrs. Jenner.

"Sure. So what? She likes to sew."

Clearly, the man was on the defensive, but before any more was said, the reporter and Grover strode out of the room. Nancy remained out of sight until they went up the stairway and she heard Mr. Belini's voice again.

"Henri will be at the Crystal Party tomorrow night," the man said. Then there was a click as he put down the telephone.

Obviously, he had called someone. Nancy stood stock-still, hoping to hear more, but the man made no other calls. She decided it would be better for her to try and follow the two men, rather than eavesdrop on Belini, so she hurried up the stairs and out the door.

Her eyes roamed the street, but the pair was nowhere in sight! They couldn't have gone too far on the ice, Nancy reasoned. They must have taken a taxi.

Disappointed, she headed back to the restaurant, digging in her rubberized heels to avoid slipping. On the way, she picked up a newspaper. When she arrived, Bess and George were not there.

After the two girls had seen Russell Kaiser leave in the police car, they assumed that he was on his way to the local precinct.

"Let's go there," George suggested. "Maybe we'll get a chance to talk to him."

The girls asked the doorman for the address. He gave it to them but said, "I wouldn't recommend bothering poor Mr. Kaiser now. He's very upset, as you can well imagine."

"Don't worry," George said. "We only want to talk to him because we might be able to help him."

The doorman raised his eyebrows and was about to ask them how, but the girls just smiled sweetly and left.

When they arrived at the police station, they did not see the bald-headed man. Upon asking at the desk, they learned he was talking to the captain, but would be done in a few minutes. Bess and George sat down to wait.

"I bet Nancy has eaten our lunch as well as hers by now," Bess murmured to her cousin.

"I just hope she's still there," George said. "Of course, Millington may only give her a half hour off, in which case she's probably left."

The cousins' conversation ended abruptly as Mr. Kaiser appeared. The girls stood up quickly.

"Mr. Kaiser," George said when he strode toward them.

He paused.

"Remember us? We met you at the Speers' auction the other evening," Bess continued.

"Oh, yes," he said now. "You were with the young lady who bid on the medallion."

"Yes. We saw the news item about the burglary and wondered if the medallion had been stolen, too."

"You followed me here to ask me that?" he replied, incredulous.

"We're detectives," Bess said.

"Amateur detectives," George added. "May we speak to you a moment? We have some information that might be of interest to you."

Kaiser shrugged. "Why not?"

Without revealing too much about the mysteries they were working on with their friend, Nancy Drew, George explained their special concern for the distinctive medallion.

"It's very possible," she declared, "that the man who was bidding on it is the burglar you're looking for. He told us he was you."

"Not only that," Bess spoke up, "but he seemed to want that medallion an awful lot."

"Enough to steal it, I suppose," Mr. Kaiser said with a glint of mischief.

"Exactly," Bess said.

"Well, girls, I appreciate the clues, but I'm afraid you're on the wrong track. You see, the robber wasn't the least bit interested in the medallion. I had put it in the safe with some other things that he took. He left the medallion, though, probably thinking it was a valueless trinket."

The girls were disappointed. "Then obviously the burglar wasn't the man who competed with you at the auction," George said. "But why did he introduce himself to us as Russell Kaiser?"

Mr. Kaiser shrugged. "I have no idea, and to be quite honest, I don't really care. Now, I have other matters to take care of. If you will excuse me, please."

He hurried off, and the young detectives left the precinct and headed for the restaurant. To their relief, they found Nancy still there, dallying over a salad.

"We thought for sure you'd be gone by now," Bess said as she and George sat down. "What happened to your job at Millington?"

"I have no job," Nancy replied, spearing a piece of lettuce with her fork, "but I do have lots of other news."

She told about her encounters, the conversations she had overheard, and her current suspicions.

"I'm convinced Ted Henri deliberately tried to send me off on another mystery—" Nancy said.

"The auction scheme," George put in.

"Right—because he didn't want me near the case involving Mr. Reese."

"And Jacqueline's been helping her brother," Bess remarked.

"Then her story about the kidnapping was phony," George added.

"I'm not positive about that," Nancy said. "Maybe she really did believe her brother was missing. Otherwise, why didn't she appear for the fashion show? What makes less sense is that she turned up at the hotel later."

"Also, we never did see her and Ted together

at any time that evening," George added.

"Exactly. So it's possible that someone wanted her to believe Ted had been kidnapped," Nancy concluded. "Someone who was determined to keep her away long enough to steal those expensive gowns!"

After the young detective's idea took root in everyone's mind, the other girls related their experiences of the morning.

"I'm glad the medallion wasn't stolen, for Mr. Kaiser's sake," Nancy said. "And it proves that Pete Grover wasn't the thief."

George nodded. "If Grover is working with Ted Henri, and now we have ample proof that he is, I'm sure he's not a burglar. Yet, he has a criminal record—he's wanted for check forgery. I can't figure it out."

"Neither can I," Nancy admitted.

"And why would he pretend to be Russell Kaiser?" Bess asked.

"Well, if his job at the auction was to set us up for a fake mystery, maybe he'd done some research. Found out about the Kaisers, their family's lion crest, and the names of surviving members he gleaned from Galen Kaiser's recent obituary," Nancy said.

"Then he and Henri wrote the note to Jacqueline, using the crest as a symbol," Bess added.

"But what was all that business about a crooked auction?" George put in.

"Just a ploy to make the newspaper announcement about the sale of the Kaiser estate even more tantalizing," Nancy replied.

"And all of this to keep us away from their case," George sighed. "I bet if we had combined forces we'd have solved it by now!"

"Whatever we do," Nancy said, "I don't think we should let on to Jacqueline or Ted that we know what's going on."

"Three can play pretend as easily as two," George said, trying to sound less anxious than she was.

"And tomorrow night we're going to get our chance," Nancy replied.

15

Stylist Trouble

Nancy's announcement made both George and Bess stare at her in surprise.

"What do you mean?" Bess asked.

"We're going to the Crystal Party," Nancy replied.

"The what?"

Nancy laughed, then repeated Mr. Belini's telephone conversation. "Ted Henri will be there, and it must have some significance. I think we'll be able to pick up a clue there."

"Where is it?" George inquired.

"I bought a newspaper on the way back from the fabric store, figuring there might be an announcement about it." Nancy turned to a page listing future social events and handed it to her friends.

"'The Crystal Party,'" Bess read aloud. "'Highlight of the fashion year. Every major designer represented. Tickets two hundred and fifty dollars. Advance reservations only.'"

"Well, that lets me out," George mumbled. "Who can afford it, anyway?"

Nancy giggled. "Lots of people," she said.

"Only the crème de la crème," Bess said, adding, "and Miss Nancy Drew, perhaps."

"Now, now," the young detective said, "I have a hunch we can go to the party without paying a penny."

"Sure, if we sneak in," Bess said. "I could disguise myself as Lady Macaroni and you could be Baroness von Hootenanny!"

"Even if we could wangle invitations, we'd have to wear the same things we wore to the benefit," George put in, "and I spilled salad dressing on my gown."

"See, it's hopeless," Bess insisted.

"On the contrary." Nancy smiled. "We are going to be the three most eligible young ladies there and in the three most beautiful gowns! C'mon!"

The girls paid the bill and trailed outside, letting Nancy lead the way. Salt trucks had spread the melting grains on the street and a similar layer covered the sidewalk, so Bess was able to keep pace as the trio walked up the street.

"Where are we going?" she asked Nancy.

"To Reese Associates, of course."

"Oh, boy. I hope Mr. Reese is in a better mood than the one we left him in," George commented.

"I hope so, too, because I'd like to persuade him to take us to the Crystal Party."

To the girls' relief, the man's temper had subsided. He even seemed unusually happy, judging by his enthusiastic welcome.

"I just received some very exciting news! Come into my office," he said, adding as they took seats. "Zoe Babbitt has decided to buy everything you modeled the other night, Nancy. Can you imagine? Everything!"

"Congratulations," the visitors chimed in together.

"She said it didn't matter one bit that most of the designs might have been scooped by another dress house," the man went on. "There's nothing like a Reese original, she told me."

"So you were worrying unnecessarily," George said.

"Well, I still don't know how my other clients

134

will feel, but it's nice to know I haven't lost Mrs. Babbitt."

"Will she be at the Crystal Party?" Nancy inquired.

"Most certainly, and wearing one of my winter creations, I suspect."

"Speaking of winter creations," Nancy continued, "we came by today for a reason."

The man perked up his ears. "Is it my turn to ask what *you've* discovered?"

Nancy smiled. "Well, we've discovered some facts, but it's really too early to discuss them." She was worried that the temperamental designer might inadvertently slip something to the wrong people.

But Reese's curiosity was aroused. "Well, what exactly *did* you find out?" he pressed the girl.

"As I said, I can't tell you yet."

"Can't tell me?" he bristled. "But *I'm* the man who—"

"Mr. Reese," George interposed, "it's important to keep things confidential—for now."

"Tomorrow night could produce the final chapter," Bess added.

Seizing the chance, Nancy quickly expressed how crucial it was for the young detectives to attend the Crystal Party.

"I can arrange that easily. On one condition, though," Mr. Reese bargained. "That you tell me everything."

"I promise," Nancy smiled. "After the party."

The man grumbled in annoyance, but finally agreed to obtain invitations. "And what are you planning to wear?" he inquired.

"I suppose my old green skirt and blouse," Nancy said.

George mentioned her dress with the oily stains on it and Bess shrugged helplessly.

"Well, you can't go to the Crystal Party looking like Cinderellas before the ball," Mr. Reese said. He strode to the doorway, addressing a secretary. "Find Rosalind for me."

Nancy was surprised to hear that Rosalind had been rehired by Mr. Reese after he fired her and she went to work for Millington. Now the young detective was doubly happy she hadn't revealed her discoveries to Reese!

Soon Rosalind appeared. She returned the girls' hellos with a silent nod, then glanced at the designer. "Yes, Mr. Reese?"

"You remember Miss Drew?" the designer said to her.

"Of course," she murmured.

Nancy tried not to seem too obvious about her examination of the woman's face, which contained thin lines and shadows under the small eyes. The skin was paste white, giving her a sickly appearance.

Mr. Reese instructed Rosalind to bring in several gowns. "One for each of the girls," he told her.

Without inquiring about size, she looked at them from head to toe, then hurried out of the room.

"She's a whiz," the designer commented.

"I thought you fired her," Nancy couldn't resist saying.

"I did, but she came back."

"On her own volition?" Nancy asked.

"Well, I didn't get down on my hands and knees, if that's what you're insinuating."

Nancy ignored the comment as Rosalind reappeared with a variety of silks, taffetas, and velvets.

"Those are fine," Mr. Reese said to the assistant. "Now help them make selections."

"That one's gorgeous!" Bess exclaimed, eyeing a royal-blue taffeta dress with a broad ruffle around the bodice. "May I try it on?"

Rosalind was already leading the girls to a cubby of dressing rooms. "You can't leave here unless you do," she said.

While Nancy and George settled on their

choices, Bess was trying to zip up the narrow waist.

"I was almost positive this would fit you," the stylist said to her.

"I'm flattered—really flattered," Bess squeaked as the woman forced the zipper to close. "Only problem is, I can't breathe!"

"I can fix that," Rosalind said, tapping her fingers on her chin.

"You can?" Bess said hoarsely. "Right away?"

Instantly, the woman pulled the zipper down and the girl let out a heavy sigh. "How are you both doing?" she called out cheerfully to her friends.

"Fine," Nancy and George replied, but in fact they were having similar difficulties.

All the clothes were much too tight, George's more so than anyone's. The narrow silk skirt she had chosen hugged her ankles, forcing her to take birdlike steps.

"I'd never catch a thief in this thing!" she laughed, poking her head into Nancy's cubicle.

"Me neither!" Nancy giggled. She gazed at her elegant ivory gown with a skirt that fell in a mass of folds.

"Everything needs work," Rosalind admitted, looking at each girl in turn.

One by one, she fitted them, sticking pins along seams.

"Ouch!" Bess cried as a pin slipped through the zipper into her skin.

"Be careful, Rosalind," Mr. Reese told her from the other room. "After all, these young ladies are my personal detectives!"

With that, the woman overturned a box of pins on the floor. She fumbled, and nervously put them back. When she finished her work, she announced that the dresses would be delivered to the girls the next afternoon.

"I will give your names to the chairperson so you won't have to buy tickets," Mr. Reese said. "I assume you know where the party is being held. I will meet you there—if that's all right."

"Great," Nancy said gaily. "Thanks for everything!"

"I'm just sorry we can't invite Dave, Burt, and Ned," Bess said when they reached Aunt Eloise's apartment house.

"Next time," Nancy remarked.

"Humph—next time," Bess pouted.

But as morning came and the sun shone over a glaze of snow that had fallen during the night, she regained her old enthusiasm.

"I'm really going to pamper myself today," Bess declared, fluffing her curls.

"Considering it could be a long evening," Nancy said, "I think that's a terrific idea—for all of us!"

Despite the fact the threesome chose to stay inside all day, the hours flew quickly. When Aunt Eloise arrived home from shopping, it was already late afternoon and the altered dresses had not yet arrived!

"Maybe we should call Mr. Reese's office," Bess suggested.

Nancy dialed the number, but a voice told her that the designer had left early.

"Is Rosalind there?" the girl inquired.

"Just a minute, please."

After a long pause, the voice returned.

"No, I'm sorry. She isn't here, either."

George spoke as Nancy hung up the receiver. "Well, it's back to salad stains," she said. But a few minutes later, the buzzer from downstairs signaled the delivery.

"Thank goodness!" Bess said, when she saw the gowns in plastic bags.

The girls immediately removed them and disappeared into the bedroom to change. But as they pulled on the small metal tabs to open the long zippers, they discovered tiny stitches around the teeth.

The dresses had been sewn up tight!

16

Undercover Disguise

The three girls stared at the gowns in horror.

"What are we going to do?" Bess gasped.

Nancy quickly asked her aunt if she had a pair of small scissors.

"Or three pairs?" George added.

"All I have are these," the woman replied, removing tiny shears from a sewing basket and large ones from a desk drawer, "and I'm afraid you might cut a hole in the material, if you use the big pair."

"We don't have much time," Nancy said, "so I'll have to take the chance."

While the cousins went to work with the small blades, Nancy slipped the longer ones under the top threads that held the zipper of her dress. She cut through stitch after stitch until she reached the metal base that seemed miles from where she had started. It was only after the threesome had finished the arduous job that they took a moment to talk.

"Who would do such a thing?" Bess said as she hurried to change. "Not Rosalind, I'm sure."

"You never know," Nancy said thoughtfully, remembering Rosalind's connection with Millington. But since the alterations turned out to be done properly, she concluded that Bess was probably right.

"Well, somebody didn't want us to go to the Crystal Party tonight," George said, combing her hair as quickly as she could.

"But whoever it was didn't count on three fine seamstresses." Aunt Eloise laughed.

The girls paraded in front of her, bringing a sigh of contentment from the woman.

"Now that's how I like to see you all—going off to a lovely party," she said. "No dangerous mission, I hope." There was a tone of uncertainty in her voice.

"As long as we stick together," Nancy assured her, "we'll be okay."

"Uh-oh," Aunt Eloise said. "Does that mean you do expect trouble?"

"I don't expect anything," the girl detective said, winking. "'Bye."

When the trio arrived at the hall where the

party was being held, they were completely awestruck by the decorations. Fine, dainty snowflakes and crystal stars hung from the ceiling that overlooked an array of birch trees with silvery branches. Mirrors on dinner tables glowed from candlelit centerpieces that carried out the winter theme.

"It's a fairyland," Nancy said, as women in stunning evening clothes and men in tuxedos mingled animatedly.

"There's Mr. Reese," Bess commented, "and that must be his wife. Wow!"

The designer spotted the girls at the same time and came forward, introducing Sheila.

"She left our house in Florida just to come up for this party," he said, explaining the woman's deep tan.

"Richard has told me a lot about you all," she smiled, her teeth as glistening as her sleek, white gown.

But before the conversation could continue, another woman called her away, leaving Mr. Reese with the three girls. He led them through the crowd, pausing to make introductions.

"I know Reese creations when I see them," declared one man, handsome with a long cap of white hair. "Aren't you going to tell me who these mystery ladies are, Richard?"

But the designer pretended not to hear and joined two other men less than a foot away. The girls, however, hung back to talk with the white-haired man. They practically froze when he announced his name.

"I'm Arnaud Hans," he said.

The designer under whose name the Reese gowns had appeared in the Chalmers catalog! No wonder Mr. Reese had ignored him!

When the young detectives finally gave their names, Hans seemed to recognize Nancy's.

"I've been hearing about you, Miss Drew, that you are doing investigative work for Richard. Well, I want to go on record that I didn't steal anything from him. He blasted me on the phone the other day, claiming that I had taken some of his spring designs and sold them to Chalmers. It's not true and I can prove it. I have dated copies of every sketch!"

Nancy was careful not to say too much, but conceded that it was not impossible for the men to have come up with the same ideas.

"Personally, I don't think Millington stole anything from him, either," Hans went on. "Other people simply created similar designs before Reese did and he's angry about it. That's all. His pride and ego are hurt because he knows he's slipping."

"I don't think he's slipping at all," Bess said in Mr. Reese's defense. "I love this dress."

"Yes, well, it is pretty, but I think it's last year's," Hans replied maliciously.

The discussion ended abruptly as Nancy edged the girls away.

"Where are we going?" Bess asked.

"To see Russell Kaiser," Nancy said.

"Mr. Kaiser's here?" the cousins replied in astonishment.

"Not the real one," their friend whispered. "Ted Henri's buddy, Pete Grover. Here he comes."

When he saw the trio, he greeted them with enthusiasm. "What a pleasant surprise," he said.

"We read about the burglary," George put in.

"Burglary?" the man stumbled.

"Yes, in your apartment," Bess said.

"Oh, oh, of course, *that* burglary." He laughed nervously. "Let's not talk about such a dreary subject," he said. "As a matter of fact, Nancy, I had planned to give you a call about the man who bought my uncle's medallion at Speers."

"You have a lead on him?" Nancy inquired.

"No," the man replied. "But I wanted to find out if you knew anything."

"Well, I haven't spoken to him since that evening," Nancy said, "but I think I know where to find him."

"You do? Oh—that's wonderful. You must tell me all about him. But first let me talk to my friend Bob over there. I've been trying to get hold of him all evening. I'll be back in a few minutes."

With that, Grover turned and was quickly swallowed up by the crowd. The girls were convinced he had just used his friend as an excuse and that he would try to avoid them for the rest of the evening.

A moment later Nancy caught sight of Grover behind a silver birch tree again. Another man in a tuxedo was with him. Wondering who he was, Nancy darted away from the cousins, but was stopped short by Sheila Reese's long, braceleted arm.

"Where are you off to in such a hurry?" the designer's wife asked. "Come, I'd like you to meet some friends of ours."

Nancy did not wish to appear rude, so she followed the woman to a table where her husband and another couple were seated. Bess and George had witnessed the diversion, and to Nancy's relief, went to follow Grover instead. A few moments later, however, they joined the group at the table.

"We lost him," George whispered when they sat down.

"Don't worry," Nancy whispered back. "At least you tried."

Just then her elbow accidentally pushed against a glass of water and it fell.

"Oh!" Nancy cried, quickly righting the glass, but not before several drops had trailed onto her lap. "Excuse me a moment," she said, popping up to go to a powder room, while Mr. Reese stared dishearteningly at the water mark on the precious skirt.

When Nancy emerged from the powder room, she did not return to the table right away. Instead, she wandered around until she finally saw Pete Grover and his companion again. Although their backs were to her, she could see their faces clearly in a panel of mirrors on the wall. The second man was Ted Henri, otherwise known as Chris Chavez! They were looking at their watches as if something were about to happen.

Nancy pulled as close as she could without being observed by either of them, and tried to overhear their conversation. The din of voices in the room, however, seemed louder than ever; and all she was able to catch was Gramercy Park and the number "11." Did it refer to an address or to the time?

No further clarification came as the men were whisked onto the dance floor by two women friends. Nancy hurried back to the Reese table, but no one was there. She scanned the couples who were dancing but saw neither of her friends.

"Where are they?" Nancy murmured, wishing she could tell Bess and George what she had learned.

But they seemed to have disappeared, and in less than twenty minutes it would be eleven o'clock, the hour when Nancy might find the solution to the puzzle. Instantly, she made her decision. She hurried to the check room to get her wrap and left a detailed message for the cousins, then darted out into the street and hailed a taxi.

The snow that had fallen earlier had melted entirely, leaving only a light dampness underfoot, which Nancy appreciated as she reached Gramercy Park. She asked the driver to let her out in front of a building several doors away from Number 11, and stepped toward an opposite canopy.

There, in the glow of a waning moon and a street lamp, she fixed her eyes on Number 11. She noticed a shadowy figure in the second-floor windows. It moved out of sight, emerging shortly in the doorway downstairs.

It was Rosalind, Mr. Reese's stylist!

17

A Four-Handed Ruse

A cold wind penetrated Nancy's cloak as she watched the woman in the doorway, who seemed to be waiting for someone. Then, as if in answer to the girl detective's curiosity, a taxi pulled up to Number 11 and Mr. Belini, the owner of the fabric store, stepped out.

At the same time Nancy noticed a van parked down the street. Its lights flashed on and off and the vehicle crawled toward the building. But the dimness of the street lamps prevented her from seeing the driver and the person sitting next to him.

On a hunch Nancy pulled the collar of her cloak high around her neck and darted to a nearby corner, circling to the back of the van as Belini moved in and out of the doorway. Her heart thumping in panic, the girl dived into the shadow of the adjoining building to watch.

Rosalind seemed to have vanished, but Belini hurried to the vehicle's rear doors. He opened one, revealing a rack of dresses covered in plastic. If only Nancy could get a closer look!

Belini poked his head deeper into the van, running through the dresses as if he were counting them. He shook his head and ran into the building once more, leaving the door ajar.

Nancy instantly raced forward, grabbing a plastic bag and pulling it into the light. As she had suspected, the gown inside was one that had been stolen the night of the benefit fashion show!

Before she could inspect the rest, however, the door opened again and she heard Belini's voice. She leaped into the van, grateful that the engine was running and muffled any noise she made.

Belini walked over to the van, then stopped to talk to the driver. This gave Nancy enough time to hide behind the rack. To her relief, there was a partition between the front and rear of the small vehicle, so no one could see her unless the dresses were removed.

Yet she had little breathing space, and the garments surrounding her created a warmth

that was uncomfortable, almost suffocating.

"Maybe this wasn't such a great idea," Nancy murmured, realizing she was trapped!

But there was no time to change her mind as the wheels of the van began to move under her!

By now Bess and George had met two young men who introduced themselves as Woody Haskins and Frank Vanderveer. Both looked to be in their twenties, and told the girls that their parents were in the clothing business. They had lived in New York City all their lives.

"And where are you two from?" Woody inquired.

"River Heights," Bess replied. "Home of the famous Nancy Drew."

"Oh, yes. She's an amateur detective," Woody said. Then he whirled Bess onto the dance floor.

"Hm-hm. So am I," Bess told him.

"You solve mysteries, too?" Frank asked George. He was tall and seemed reserved like her friend, Burt Eddleton, which made the girl relax almost immediately.

"Oh, we all do," she said brightly, as the music picked up tempo.

The beat was faster now, and the couples fell apart from each other for the duration of the dance. Afterwards, their escorts took the girls to the buffet for a snack. When they returned to their table, Bess and George suddenly realized that Nancy hadn't come back yet.

Vaguely uneasy, they wondered what had happened to her. Bess nudged George. "We've been having such a good time that we forgot all about our best friend!" she whispered. "Where do you think Nancy went?"

"I don't know," George said, "but I think we ought to go looking for her."

The girls excused themselves and moved off, but neither of their escorts was ready to release them so quickly. The music had started again, and Frank and Woody ran after Bess and George, begging for another dance.

"But we can't stay!" Bess insisted as Woody tugged on her hand, pulling her back on the floor.

"Why not? Do you turn into a pumpkin at eleven o'clock?" The young man laughed, causing a tiny grin to wrinkle the girl's face.

"No, but we really do have to leave," Bess declared and motioned to George, who looked forlornly at her date.

When the foursome stood together again, the young men continued to plead. "You came here to enjoy yourselves, didn't you?" Frank asked.

"Why do you want to go home so early?"

"Well, we're not going home," George said. "We're investigating something."

"Tonight?" Woody and Frank chorused.

"We'll go with you," the latter volunteered.

"Oh, no!" Bess exclaimed. "It's nice of you to offer, but—"

"Then it's all settled," Frank put in. "Now tell us, what are you looking for?"

"Our friend Nancy," George said.

"Describe her," Frank went on. "Then we'll fan out and search. Afterwards, we'll meet at your table."

Bess and George were glad to have help, but when they rejoined their dates fifteen minutes later, no one had seen Nancy.

"Maybe she left the party," Woody suggested.

"Let's see if her cloak is still in the checkroom," George replied.

Upon questioning the woman in charge, the girls were given Nancy's message.

"We ought to go there at once," Frank spoke up. "Get a taxi, Woody."

In the cab, Bess whispered to George, "I'm glad we have a couple of strong men with us!"

"Just hope we find Nancy!" George said.

By the time they climbed out of the taxi at

Gramercy Park, most lights had been turned out in the various buildings and Number 11 seemed unoccupied.

"Maybe Nancy gave up on whatever she was looking for and went home," Woody suggested.

"Nancy? Give up? Never!" Bess said.

She and George hurried ahead of the men toward the iron fence that framed the park area itself, thinking they had heard someone crying. But as they drew near, they realized it was only the whine of a small puppy.

"Where could Nancy have gone?" Bess wailed.

She and George roamed close to the fence, peering at the blackness beyond, half wondering if Nancy had been abducted and taken to some forsaken area of the city.

As they returned to their escorts, who had remained near the entrance to Number 11, the cousins glimpsed something shiny in the street.

It was Nancy's earring!

"It's crushed," George said, examining it.

"Maybe a car rolled over it," Frank commented.

"Maybe one that kidnapped her!" Bess exclaimed in fright.

As she spoke, the window above slid open and a woman addressed the foursome. The cousins looked up to see who it was, but the speaker pulled back as a waft of cold air drifted in.

"I believe the girl you are looking for is here," she called out.

"Is that you, Rosalind?" George said, thinking she recognized the voice.

But there was no reply, only a halting cough.

"Should we go up?" Bess asked.

"There's nothing to be afraid of," Woody said.

"Yeah, we're with you," his friend added.

Even so, the girls wondered if the invitation was a sinister ruse. If Nancy were being held captive inside, the cousins might be stepping into the same carefully laid trap!

"Come on," Woody urged, leading the way into the dim corridor. "We have to find Nancy!"

Bess, George, and Frank followed. The sounds of their footsteps on the stairway echoed loudly through the empty building, and the girls shivered when Woody banged his fist on the door. Tensely, they waited for the woman to open it!

18

Escort Accomplices

Almost at once the door swung open, but no one was immediately visible in the plainly furnished room. Bess and George stepped inside, calling, "Nancy?"

"Maybe we're in the wrong—" George started to say when several hands grabbed her and Bess from behind and pushed them toward the opposite wall. Each had a hand clasped over their eyes, so they could not see their attackers.

"Help!" the cousins shrieked as they were shoved into a closet. A moment later, a key turned in the lock.

"Let us out of here!" Bess cried.

"They must have jumped Frank and Woody, too," George said, pressing her ear against the closet door. "I don't hear anything."

Bess listened also, but the room seemed vacant. Had their attackers subdued the two young men and taken them away, leaving the girls trapped in the stuffy closet?

"I think I'm going to faint," Bess murmured, swaying back against George.

"You can't pass out now!" the other girl exclaimed. She was ready to hurl herself full force into the door, but stopped as footsteps echoed outside.

Were their captors returning?

The cousins remained quiet, feeling a sudden fierce shiver pulse up their spines. George quickly squatted to the keyhole. It afforded only a partial view of the room, but enough to establish the identity of those in it.

Woody and Frank! She gasped.

Was it possible that she and Bess had been tricked by the young men? Had they used their charm to imprison the girls?

"What do you see?" Bess whispered.

"Sh—" her cousin said, pressing her ear under the knob to listen to the conversation.

"We'll keep them here until we get rid of the third one," George heard Woody say.

"Where is she?" Frank asked.

"In the van," Woody replied. Apparently,

she found it parked out front and walked right in. They caught her hiding behind the dresses."

Bess tapped on George's shoulder, begging to be told something, but George shook her head. She didn't want to miss anything that was being said.

"Rozzie wants us to meet her at the pier in an hour or so," Frank spoke up again, but the rest of his sentence became unintelligible as he pulled a cellophane wrapper off a cigar and crumpled it.

George was positive that "the third one" referred to Nancy, and that Rozzie was Rosalind, the stylist at Reese Associates. Had she reconciled herself to the designer merely because she needed continuing access to him? That seemed to be the case.

"Reese never should've fired Paula Jenner," Frank said, puffing on the cigar. "Those two sisters are real soul mates."

Now there was a lull as Frank strode toward the closet, letting the pungent smoke clog the keyhole.

"You alive in there?" he called out sarcastically. "Sorry we had to do this, girls."

The cousins did not answer, and George confirmed to Bess that the speaker had been her escort, Frank. The blond girl felt like crying, but George gripped her arm and motioned for her to listen.

The men, however, made only one other vague reference to the last pier at the West Side docks.

"On second thought," Woody's voice came again, "let's take a ride up there now. These two aren't going anywhere."

"They're leaving!" George whispered.

She waited until she was sure the men were out of the building, then leaned her weight against the door and flung herself back and forth several times, hoping to force the lock. It held firm, though, and the searing pain that drove through George's shoulder brought her to a halt.

"I'll do it," Bess said.

With determination, she plunged ahead, hitting the door hard. It didn't open, but it had weakened.

"I knew these few extra pounds would come in handy someday," Bess quipped, crashing forward again.

This time the tumblers snapped.

"You're fabulous!" George complimented her cousin as they raced down the stairs and out into the moistening air.

They dashed to a corner where passing cars

were visible and quickly hailed a taxi.

"Where to?" the driver asked.

"The last pier at the West Side docks," George said.

"The what?" the man gulped. "It's a little late to go swimming, isn't it?"

The cousins were not in the mood for small talk, but listened courteously as the driver continued.

"No boats leaving now, either," he said. "You girls ought to go home."

"I wish we could," Bess murmured, as a chilling breeze swept through the window crack.

"Just be glad we're out of that closet," George whispered.

"And into a frying pan?" her cousin said.

By now, the driver had guided the cab around the park and was heading across town. He kept his pace moderate, giving his passengers time to plot their moves.

"What do we do if one of us gets caught?" Bess asked her cousin.

"You mean by Frank or Woody?"

"Or by anybody else," Bess replied.

"Then the other one hops in this cab and takes off for the police station."

"Maybe we should do that now," Bess said.

"I considered it," George said, "but I really doubt we'd be able to convince an officer to come with us. He'd probably think we're just a couple of kooky teenagers."

"How could he?" Bess said, glancing at the taffeta dress that showed through her coat. "I think we look rather sophisticated."

"Well, that may be so, but New York isn't River Heights where everybody including Chief McGinnis knows us."

George's remark only reinforced her cousin's anxiety as the taxi looped in the direction of the Hudson River.

"It's pitch black out there!" Bess exclaimed.

"Sure you gals really want me to drop you at the pier?" the driver said shortly.

"If you don't mind," George replied, "we'd like you to wait."

"How long?" he asked.

"It depends," Bess put in.

"On what?"

"On what we find, of course."

"Hmm. Maybe you ought to tell me what you're looking for first."

"We're looking for our friend," George revealed. "She was kidnapped and we think she's been taken to this pier."

The man glanced at her sharply for a moment.

"And you're going to play big shots and rescue her, eh? If what you tell me is true, why didn't you call the cops?"

"I'm afraid they wouldn't have believed us," George said lamely.

"Right. They wouldn't, and neither do I."

George and Bess did not comment, and again the driver took his eyes off the street to stare at them. "Where are you from?" he inquired.

"River Heights."

"Just arrived?"

"No. We were at the Crystal Party and that's where our friend disappeared," Bess said.

The driver mumbled something as he drew up closer to the last pier building. It had a bleak, eerie atmosphere. An ice floe rocked against the dock, and except for the hazy glow of the moon, the area lay in frigid darkness.

"I guess I can't really drop you off here and leave you alone," the driver relented finally. "But it'll cost you to keep the meter running."

"That's all right. And thanks," George said, as a chugging sound from the river caused Bess to roll down her window all the way.

"Who'd be out on the river at this time of night?" she asked. The cab moved forward slowly.

"Maybe they're transporting stolen dresses

somewhere," George suggested excitedly, and asked the driver to turn off his headlights.

"Oh, now we're playing cops and robbers in the dark!" he grumbled, but complied with the request.

For a moment, everyone listened as the chugging sound of the boat diminished to a low, even hum.

"It's gone," Bess declared at last. "We'll probably never know what it was here for. Maybe we ought to go back to Aunt Eloise's."

"Good idea," the driver agreed, glancing at the number on his meter. "I can think of better ways to make money!"

He pressed the accelerator lightly and switched on the headlights again. As he swung the cab away from the building, the cousins caught sight of a van parked by a wire fence alongside the pier. A blue car stood behind it.

"Oh, please pull up farther," George begged.

"By that van?" the driver asked.

"Just before it."

He did, and the young detective quickly climbed out of the taxi. Leaving Bess to wait, George raced to the vehicle.

I wonder if this is the one Woody and Frank mentioned, she said to herself, the one in which Nancy was discovered?

Cautiously, George pulled down the handle on the rear door and opened it. A lump formed in her throat as she gazed inside. In the gleam of the taxi's headlights, she saw a heap of black wool. It was Nancy's evening cloak!

She signaled to Bess, then motioned toward the pier building. The entrance bore a sign reading: CLOSED. But a sliver of light was visible underneath the door.

Bess got out of the cab and hurried to join her cousin. "We've got to call the police!" she urged.

"But we don't have time!" George argued.

Bess's heels sank in a layer of gravel and a shiver of fear shot down her spine. "If we go in," she said, "they'll take all of us!"

19

Flaming Rescue

But George paid no attention to her cousin's warning. Instead, with a decisive motion, she slid her hand around the latch and lifted it noiselessly, opening the door a crack.

George peered through, then pulled back with a gulp. "Oh, my goodness!"

"What is it?" Bess whispered.

"Racks of clothes. Here, see for yourself!"

Bess pressed her face against the crack, then said under her breath, "I bet the gang converted this old building into a warehouse, or 'drop' for garments, before distributing them."

"Looks like it," George agreed.

"What are we going to do?" Bess asked.

"We'll have to go in! Nancy might be tied up somewhere!"

"But you know the gang's in there! The

people who came with the van, and I bet Woody and Frank arrived in that car! Also, Rosalind might be around."

"Look, we'll have to take that chance. It's a big place, and if we're careful, they'll never realize we're here." Silently, George crept through the door, not giving Bess another opportunity to object.

Together they ducked behind the nearest rack and listened. Everything was quiet, and after a minute or so, George signaled for her cousin to follow her.

The young detectives tiptoed between racks that contained mostly imported merchandise, searching anxiously for a sign of Nancy or their enemies. But all they found was clothing!

Suddenly, George came to a sudden halt. "Hey!" she called in a whisper, and pointed to a gown that was hanging on a hook without plastic covering. "Isn't that the dress Nancy wore tonight?"

Bess bobbed her head as she noticed a smudge of makeup on the ivory neckline. "It's—"

She was interrupted by the shuffle of feet some distance away.

"Over there!" George said, indicating a stack of cartons along the wall.

The girls edged forward, careful not to clack their heels on the cement floor. Their blood was pumping hard and fast as they heard Frank's voice.

"Hey, Woody! I heard a noise. Someone's in here!"

Another set of footsteps approached, then Woody replied, "Did you see anyone?"

"No, but I heard something rustle."

"All right. You take one side and I'll take the other. We'll check it out."

Bess and George had reached the stack of boxes and squatted down, each girl pulling a large carton over herself.

I hope they don't move any of this stuff, George thought fearfully. Bess almost gasped when one of the men walked past the box she was in, but then the footfalls died away again.

"Must've been a rat," the girls heard Woody say. "Come on, let's finish the inventory and count the stuff that just came in so we can go home."

The two men moved away to another part of the warehouse, and the cousins slowly extricated themselves from their hiding places.

"What'll we do now?" Bess asked. "We can't stay here. Those guys might come back any minute."

George had spotted a door straight ahead. "Maybe Nancy's in there." She surveyed the narrow path between the wall and a pile of paraphernalia lying near it. There was enough room for her to walk through without touching anything, but Bess wore a crinoline under her taffeta skirt, and any contact would make more noise!

"Bess, take your slip off," she advised. "Otherwise you'll hit a million things with your skirt and they'll hear us."

Glancing down the row of boxes, mirrors, and rolls of seamless paper commonly used as backdrops by photography studios like Zanzibar's, the girl knew she had no choice. It was an obstacle course she would have to clear unhindered.

As quickly as she could, she unhooked the waist of her slip and let it fall. Then carefully, she tiptoed after her cousin. George reached for the doorknob and turned it slowly.

To her relief, the door opened without resistance, and they found themselves in a small, windowless room illuminated by a single light bulb hanging from the ceiling. On the floor were more storage cartons and some empty racks. And, beside one of the large boxes lay Nancy Drew, wearing a plain cotton dress. Her hands and feet were bound, and she was gagged!

"Nancy!" Bess cried out, falling to her feet and struggling to free the girl.

George was looking for a pair of scissors to cut Nancy's bonds, when suddenly she heard footsteps again. They sounded like a woman's and were coming closer!

She motioned for Bess to be silent, then flattened herself against the wall, waiting for the door to swing open.

The footsteps stopped in front, as if the person were reluctant to enter. Then the door opened and Rosalind stepped in!

Instantly, the cousins grabbed her, and George clapped a hand over the stylist's mouth before Rosalind could utter a scream. At the same time, she kicked the door shut.

"Let—me—go!" Rosalind managed to whimper through George's hand.

"Not yet!" the girl said, while Bess snatched a wad of material from one of the boxes and stuffed it into the woman's mouth. George removed her rope belt, using it to tie Rosalind's wrists, and forced the stylist to the floor.

Bess sat on her legs, letting George tackle the bindings on Nancy that were only partially loose. George ripped at the thick knot behind the girl's head, splitting a fingernail as the tight loops opened and the gag fell away.

"Thanks!" Nancy said hoarsely. "What happened to the two guys who dumped me here?"

"I don't know," George replied. "All I know is that our ex-dates are here, Woody Haskins and Frank Vanderveer."

"Your ex-dates?" Nancy asked, bewildered.

"And they seemed so nice, too," George grumbled. "Woody was so handsome, with a bit of gray in his hair, even though he was only in his twenties—"

"Was the rest of it dark and did he have small features?" Nancy asked excitedly.

"Why, yes—"

"He must be the guy I saw snooping around the dressing rooms after the fashion show!" Nancy exclaimed. "Apparently, he came back for some reason after the clothes had been stolen. Maybe he lost something. How did you meet these people?"

"I think we should explain later and get out of here as fast as we can," Bess advised.

Rosalind, meanwhile, tried to kick her legs out from under Bess, but to no avail.

"Quit it!" Bess told the woman, who grunted angrily.

By now Nancy was free and she swayed to her feet, still feeling a twinge of pain where the cord had been tightened against her skin.

"Can you walk?" Bess asked anxiously.

"I think so," Nancy replied.

Ted Henri and Pete Grover had left the Crystal Party shortly after Nancy did. On a lead that Mr. Belini had inadvertently revealed to them, they had driven to Gramercy Park. By the time they arrived, however, the small van with Nancy inside had left, and they saw Belini step into a car with another man. Neither Ted nor his associate recognized the stranger.

"Let's see what they're up to," Ted said, putting his car into gear.

The men ahead of them seemed unaware that they were being followed. They moved through the darkened streets, aiming toward an all-night diner on the West Side. As they pulled into the parking lot, Ted let his car hum idly a moment, then swung in behind.

"We'll give them time to sit down before we go in," he told his companion.

"Belini will recognize us," Pete Grover warned.

"Well, I'm hoping he won't see us."

They sat in the car watching the two men slide into a high-backed booth near a window.

"Okay?" Ted said. "Let's go."

He and Pete hurried inside and found a vacant booth behind Belini, where they strained to hear the conversation between Belini and his confederate. "Listen, Iannone, you shouldn't have quit Millington," Belini was saying. "We need you there."

"It wasn't my idea, believe me. It was Rosalind's," Iannone said. "The minute Nancy Drew walked into the place, Rozzie panicked."

"Oh, baloney," Belini grumbled. "Rozzie's just overly worried about getting caught. Now she's back with Reese and you're out of a job."

"Look, it's only temporary. We worked a deal or two with Millington. Once I get situated with a new company, we'll be able to create interest there, too." Iannone paused, letting out a big sigh. "Meantime, I'm available to help you deliver the imported goods. They're down at the pier now, right?"

Belini nodded, then he let his fist fall on the table. "I still can't figure out why you offered that snoopy kid a job to begin with."

"I was trapped, that's all. I tried to dissuade her from working at Millington, but she gave her reasons. They all had to do with collecting inside information, which would ultimately point the finger at someone and free the company from unjust attacks by Reese. What could I say? I was supposed to be a loyal, trustworthy employee!"

Belini snorted.

"Anyhow," Iannone went on, "I figured, with Rosalind's help, we could keep Nancy Drew in check. But Rozzie made a mistake. She rigged a blackout on the floor, and locked Nancy Drew in right after I hired her, hoping to scare her away."

"That was dumb," Belini agreed.

"It was—because it made me look suspicious. I told Rosalind that, and she suggested that we both quit Millington permanently. When everything dies down, I could try to go back, but I don't think it's such a hot idea."

"It isn't," Belini agreed. "Well, let's finish our coffee and get out of here. It's late."

Quickly, Ted and Pete left the diner. They moved the car so it pointed toward the street, shut off the ignition, and waited for the men.

"Nancy Drew's quite persistent, isn't she?" Ted said.

"I hate to say I told you so," Pete replied, "but I doubted right from the start that the fake auction scheme would keep her off this case."

"My sister said the same thing. All I know is,

it's too bad that those crooks got to Jackie the night of the fashion show. Otherwise, I might never have had to introduce myself to Nancy as Chris Chavez."

"What exactly happened?" Pete asked.

"Well, one of these guys told Jackie that they had kidnapped me, and they'd let me go if she agreed not to be in the fashion show. They knew I was after a story involving them and that she was supposed to model clothes they intended to steal.

"Jackie, of course, is no idiot. She insisted they let her see me before she would make such an agreement. So they told her to go to some building and the next thing she knew, she was blindfolded and pushed into somebody's basement."

"Obviously, she got out unharmed," Pete commented.

"Obviously, but not before I turned up at the fashion show and discovered Nancy Drew in her place. Of course, I didn't know who she was at first. I even thought she might have been planted by the crooks. So I asked her to dance, hoping to ingratiate myself enough to keep tabs on her in the future."

Pete laughed. "Not an easy thing to do with Nancy."

"Exactly. When I realized who she was, I knew I had to do more than that. A meddlesome teenager would not help my investigation."

"And so you sent her off on a wild-goose chase."

"That's right," Ted concluded.

Back at the pier, the young detectives had managed to restrain Rosalind, but now they heard their captors' voices outside the small room. Even though the men did not know what had happened, they were cutting off the girls' escape route!

"I wish Rozzie would get over here to help us count this stuff," Frank grumbled. "Without some assistance, we'll be here all night!"

"Last time I saw her, she was going to check on Nancy Drew. Why don't you see what's holding her up?"

Frank approached the door, but suddenly stopped dead in his tracks as police sirens sounded outside.

"The cops!" he yelled. "Let's get out of here! Roz, are you in there?" he shouted toward the room. When he received no answer, he ran to the door and locked it. Then he darted after his companion.

Everything was quiet for a few minutes until

Bess spoke up. "I don't hear the sirens anymore, and the police haven't come into the building, either. Do you think they just happened to drive by?"

George shrugged. "Could be. There's a phone on the wall over there. Why don't we call the precinct?"

Nancy instantly picked up the receiver, but the line was dead. Fighting a wave of panic, she realized they were locked up in an abandoned warehouse and might not be found for days!

"How about these?" Bess asked, handing Nancy a pair of scissors.

She attempted to free the lock with them, but had no luck.

"Let's try to break the door," she suggested, forcing herself to stay calm.

Nancy and the cousins threw their weight against the wood several times, but it wouldn't even crack. Finally they stopped, rubbing their bruises and taking deep breaths.

"What are we going to do?" Bess moaned.

"I suppose we'll have to wait for someone to find us," Nancy said. "I—" She stopped suddenly, sniffing the air. Smoke was seeping in under the door!

"The building's on fire!" Nancy cried out.

20

The Last Twist

Rosalind made noises through her gag, trying to indicate a spot on the wall where several overalls hung on a hook. Nancy removed the garments, and found a key hanging behind them.

With shaking hands, she inserted it into the lock. To her great relief, it worked!

Instantly, the girls pulled Rosalind to her feet, took the gag out, and dragged her along out the door. Tongues of fire were lapping over the racks of clothing, spreading quickly and threatening the group's escape.

Nevertheless, they hurried on bravely. The young detectives covered their mouths and kept their heads low. Rosalind, however, allowed the rising heat to bite her face and the

smoke to settle in her throat as they ran toward the entrance.

Flames had torn through the door by now and the girl could not get out without being injured. Nancy looked for another exit, but none seemed to exist!

Would they all be consumed by the fire?

As the frightening thought occurred to everyone, a blast of water suddenly shot through the door. Then another blast, and another!

The girls quickly ducked out of range, knowing the pressure of the deluge could sweep them back into the raging flames.

"Are you all right?" Nancy asked Rosalind, whose eyes were flooded with tears.

The woman gulped back the smoke in her mouth, coughing hard, and nodded.

Then a man kicked in the door and called for them to come out.

Nancy's eyes were smarting, but she clearly saw Ted Henri near a fire truck. He and Pete Grover were talking to police officers who had laid handcuffs on Woody, Frank, Belini, and another man whose back was to Nancy.

When she stepped in front of him, she gasped. "Mr. Iannone!" she cried.

"He was the go-between at the Millington Company," the reporter explained as someone slipped Nancy's cloak over her shoulders.

She looked at him with narrowed eyes. "And what were you, Mr. Ted Henri, alias Chris Chavez?"

"Then you knew—"

"Of course! I admit I didn't figure out the ruse right away, but when I ran into the real Chris Chavez, and Bess and George overheard your conversation with Jacqueline, not to mention the one I overheard between you and Belini, I figured it all out."

"Including the Galen Kaiser story?"

"That's right. My friends went to check the mug shots for the man who turned out to be the real Russell Kaiser, and found instead a picture of your friend Pete Grover over here!"

"Pete Grover?" Ted stared at Nancy, then at his companion.

"I do look like him, don't I?" the man asked with a grin.

"Are you telling me you're not Pete Grover, who's wanted for check forgery in California?"

"No. That's my cousin. I'm Alan Grover, and I work in the garment industry. That's why Ted asked me to help him on this case. He needed an inside man."

"Oh, I'm sorry," Nancy apologized.

"That's all right." Grover smiled. "A pretty

girl like you can make a crook out of me any day."

"How did you know about Galen Kaiser?" Nancy asked quickly, hiding her embarrassment.

"Oh, I read his obituary. Then, when the real Russell Kaiser started to bid on the medallion that had belonged to his uncle, I put in a counterbid to attract your attention. I figured he really wanted the piece, and I wouldn't be taking too much of a risk competing for it."

Nancy chuckled. "That's what I thought, until I almost had to part with several hundred dollars!"

George and Bess, who had been explaining to the police about Rosalind's capture, now came up to the group.

"It wasn't very nice to send us on a wild-goose chase," George said to Ted, drawing a sigh from the man.

"I know. I'm sorry, really I am," he replied, and dug his heels into the gravelly soil. "If it weren't for you, Nancy, I might never have wound up this story."

The girl bit her lips in a smile.

"The fact is," Ted continued, "I heard about your visit to the Millington office."

"Am I right that Rosalind went to work there

after she left Reese Associates, then quit Millington, along with Mr. Iannone?"

"Yes. She was afraid you'd find out too much too soon. Obviously, she didn't want you to poke around Millington, figuring you would discover information about her deal with Iannone."

"I gather that they were using this pier building as a drop for clothes—smuggled imports, mostly—which would be sold to a dress house like Millington. Since they were smuggled, there were no export taxes to pay." Nancy laughed. "So they were priced lower than clothes made by manufacturers in the States."

"You really do amaze me, Nancy," Ted said admiringly. "Anything else I ought to know?"

"Just that I heard a boat outside the building, and I have a hunch that the two guys who tied me up inside the warehouse are on it."

"We saw the boat," Bess put in quickly. "It headed out into the river."

Nancy advised her and George to report their observations to the police while Ted Henri nodded his head.

"As much as I hate to admit it," he said, "I think all the accolades belong to you, Nancy."

"Well, I still haven't figured out everything," she said, striding toward the prisoners who were about to depart in two patrol cars.

At the same moment, she noticed a man emerge from a darkened taxi several yards away.

"The meter's still running," he said, "and nobody's even thanked me."

"For what?" Nancy asked.

"For calling the police," he replied. "Your friends stayed in that building a bit too long to suit me. I was too chicken to go in after them myself, so I buzzed my radio and somebody sent the cops. Good thing, too, 'cause they swarmed on those guys just as they started to set the fire."

"Well, we all thank you," Nancy said, giving the man a big smile. She then turned to Rosalind who was seated next to Belini in the back of the police car. "I have only one question," she said. "If you had such a good thing going with sales of cheaper merchandise, why did you steal Mr. Reese's designs and gowns? It seems to me you were trying to ruin his business."

"I was." Rosalind sneered. "He was so terrible to my sister, Paula Jenner. She had worked for him for years and then—poof—he fired her. She needed that salary badly and he took it away for no reason at all."

"But you know the man has a volatile temper," Nancy said in Reese's defense.

"Even so, I was determined to get back at him. He has made life miserable for a lot of people, including me."

Nancy recalled how the woman had cried openly when the designer had screamed at her the night of the fashion show.

"Did you sell any of his designs to Chalmers?" the girl questioned.

"Yes. Arnaud Hans agreed to use them. But he modified them a lot. There's such jealousy and competition between the men that, as much as it pleased him to scoop the designs, he wanted to change them."

As the woman revealed her story, Nancy felt pity for her and Arnaud Hans who, despite his natural talent, would lose the esteem he had earned over the years simply because of envy and greed.

The patrol cars began to move forward, and Ted Henri turned to Nancy. "Would you and your friends like a lift home?"

Bess and George accepted gratefully, while Nancy chuckled. "Are you going to figure out a way to get rid of us again?"

"Don't tell me you don't trust me." The reporter grinned. "After all, how could I share my by-line in the newspaper with you if you were to disappear? I do mean to give you the credit you deserve, Nancy Drew!"

Before they left the area, Bess and George had offered to pay the taxi driver several times the amount on the meter, but he refused.

"This trip was on me, girls," he said. "I'm just happy that you're all safe. Here's my card," he added, "in case you need another ride some day."

George laughed. "We promise it won't be anything like this one!" she exclaimed, running to Ted's car.

On the way back to Aunt Eloise's apartment, Bess mentioned Jacqueline. That prompted Ted to explain the events of the first night he had met Nancy. When she heard that he had suspected her of being planted by the crooks, she laughed.

"This sure is an initiation for me," she said.

"Into what?" asked Al Grover, who sat next to her.

"Into the inner workings of a New York reporter's mind!"

Aunt Eloise was asleep when the girls arrived, and they waited until morning before they told her about their adventures at the West Side pier.

"Oh, how awful!" Miss Drew exclaimed when she heard everything. "Your father will never forgive me, Nancy!"

"Maybe I'd better call him," Nancy said with a chuckle. "I don't want him to read about it in the newspaper!"

Before she had a chance to dial, however, the police captain phoned to inform her that the men on the boat had been caught. "That winds up the case, Nancy," he concluded. "You did a wonderful job. Your dad will be proud of you."

Nancy giggled. "He doesn't know what happened yet. I was just about to call him."

Mr. Drew was amazed by his daughter's story. When she finished speaking, he said, "You'd be interested to know that the name Kaiser appeared in a news article today."

"Russell Kaiser?" she asked, surprised.

"Yes. Seems to me it was in a syndicated column, so you'll find it in the New York papers. I have to hurry for an appointment, so we'll talk about it later."

"Thanks, Dad!"

When her father hung up, Nancy asked Aunt Eloise for the morning newspaper. She scanned it and quickly discovered a small headline, which read, KAISER GETS THE LION'S SHARE!

Excited, Nancy read the story out loud:

"'An unusual medallion was acquired by Russell Kaiser during an auction of Speers, Limited. It came from the estate of Russell's uncle, Galen Kaiser, and bore the family crest—a lion.

"'The medallion appeared to have no great value, but Russell Kaiser, who had been out of the country when the estate was turned over to the auction house, remembered a story his uncle once told him.

"'Galen Kaiser had bought a magnificent black opal during his world travels. Later he was told that opals were known to bring bad luck and that they should never belong to anyone not born in the month of October since its lucky gemstone is the opal. After some misfortune, Galen Kaiser hid the stone and did not look at it again. When he died without a will, no one in the family found the opal.'"

"Because it was hidden in the medallion!" Aunt Eloise broke in gaily.

"That's right," Nancy said. "'And it was only when Russell Kaiser went to the preview exhibit at Speers and saw the medallion with a small, boxlike clasp on the back of it that he realized the stone might be concealed inside.'"

"No wonder he kept bidding!" George said.

"And to think Nancy almost won it," Bess said, a bit dejected.

"I'm not disappointed at all." Nancy smiled. "We couldn't have afforded any bad luck on this mystery!"

When Mr. Reese heard the girls' story later, he couldn't have agreed more. "You all deserve medals of honor," he declared, "and a special celebration!"

"Even though your dresses were ruined last night?" Nancy replied. "You know, Rosalind made me put on an old cotton one so she could take the one you gave me to wear, but it was destroyed, too."

"My dear," the designer said, "what's a little silk and taffeta worth compared to your well-being and that of your friends? I owe so much to each of you and hope you will never ever have such a dangerous experience again!"

He did not realize, of course, that Nancy would soon begin a treacherous hunt through Europe in search of the *Captive Witness*.

"On the contrary." Nancy giggled. "My goal is to be a *model* detective!"

You are invited to join

THE OFFICIAL NANCY DREW ®/
HARDY BOYS ® FAN CLUB!

Be the first in your neighborhood to find out
about the newest adventures of Nancy, Frank,
and Joe in the **Nancy Drew** ®/ **Hardy Boys** ®
Mystery Reporter, and to receive your official
membership card. Just send your name, age,
address, and zip code on a postcard *only* to:

The Official Nancy Drew ®/
Hardy Boys ® Fan Club
Wanderer Books
Simon & Schuster Building
1230 Avenue of the Americas
New York, New York 10020

NANCY DREW MYSTERY STORIES®
by Carolyn Keene

You will also enjoy
THE LINDA CRAIG™ SERIES
by Ann Sheldon